PINOCCHIO

Carlo Collodi

WITHDRAWN

COLLINS

Harper Press
An imprint of HarperCollins*Publishers*
77–85 Fulham Palace Road
Hammersmith
London W6 8JB

This Harper Press paperback edition published 2012

Carlo Collodi asserts the moral right to be identified as the author of this work

A catalogue record for this book is available from the British Library

ISBN: 978-0-00-792071-6

Printed and bound in Great Britain by Clays Ltd, St Ives plc

MIX
Paper from
responsible sources
FSC
www.fsc.org
FSC® C007454

FSC™ is a non-profit international organisation established to promote the
responsible management of the world's forests. Products carrying the FSC label
are independently certified to assure consumers that they come
from forests that are managed to meet the social, economic and
ecological needs of present and future generations.

Find out more about HarperCollins and the environment at
www.harpercollins.co.uk/green

Life & Times section © HarperCollins*Publishers* Ltd
Gerard Cheshire asserts his moral rights as author of the Life & Times section
Classic Literature: Words and Phrases adapted from
Collins English Dictionary
Typesetting in Kalix by Palimpsest Book Production Limited,
Falkirk, Stirlingshire

10 9 8 7 6 5 4 3 2 1

History of Collins

In 1819, millworker William Collins from Glasgow, Scotland, set up a company for printing and publishing pamphlets, sermons, hymn books and prayer books. That company was Collins and was to mark the birth of HarperCollins Publishers as we know it today. The long tradition of Collins dictionary publishing can be traced back to the first dictionary William published in 1824, *Greek and English Lexicon*. Indeed, from 1840 onwards, he began to produce illustrated dictionaries and even obtained a licence to print and publish the Bible.

Soon after, William published the first Collins novel, *Ready Reckoner*, however it was the time of the Long Depression, where harvests were poor, prices were high, potato crops had failed and violence was erupting in Europe. As a result, many factories across the country were forced to close down and William chose to retire in 1846, partly due to the hardships he was facing.

Aged 30, William's son, William II took over the business. A keen humanitarian with a warm heart and a generous spirit, William II was truly 'Victorian' in his outlook. He introduced new, up-to-date steam presses and published affordable editions of Shakespeare's works and *Pilgrim's Progress*, making them available to the masses for the first time. A new demand for educational books meant that success came with the publication of travel books, scientific books, encyclopaedias and dictionaries. This demand to be educated led to the later publication of atlases and Collins also held the monopoly on scripture writing at the time.

In the 1860s Collins began to expand and diversify

and the idea of 'books for the millions' was developed. Affordable editions of classical literature were published and in 1903 Collins introduced 10 titles in their Collins Handy Illustrated Pocket Novels. These proved so popular that a few years later this had increased to an output of 50 volumes, selling nearly half a million in their year of publication. In the same year, The Everyman's Library was also instituted, with the idea of publishing an affordable library of the most important classical works, biographies, religious and philosophical treatments, plays, poems, travel and adventure. This series eclipsed all competition at the time and the introduction of paperback books in the 1950s helped to open that market and marked a high point in the industry.

HarperCollins is and has always been a champion of the classics and the current Collins Classics series follows in this tradition – publishing classical literature that is affordable and available to all. Beautifully packaged, highly collectible and intended to be reread and enjoyed at every opportunity.

Life & Times

The Original *Pinocchio*

As one might expect, the novel *Pinocchio* is quite different from other picture-book and animated versions, such as the Disney film of 1940. It was originally published in 1883 as *The Adventures of Pinocchio* and was written in Italian, by the children's author Carlo Collodi.

Collodi's imaginings are very akin to those of the English author Lewis Carroll, who published *Alice in Wonderland* in 1865 and *Through the Looking Glass* in 1871. Both writers indulge in ever more weird and wonderful meanderings, aware that they have given themselves license to write whatever comes into their minds by the nature of the genre they have chosen. The 18th century was a curious time for children's literature in this respect, as it was the style to take children into imaginary realms filled with anthropomorphic animals and mythical entities, as if realism were the preserve of adult literature.

In *Pinocchio*, Collodi conjured up a rather unfeeling and spiteful character in the eponymous protagonist, whom he devised as a manifestation of his own counter-conventional views on Italian society. Pinocchio is born as a boy, but – like a baby – without a moral compass, so he is disrespectful, selfish and lacking in both sympathy and empathy.

The tale begins with a rather violent slapstick routine between two characters named Maestro Cherry and Geppetto, who manage to break into verbal and then physical fights before the former gives the latter the piece of wood that will soon be carved to become Pinocchio. This sets the tone for the book in general, which is rather at odds with the traditionally accepted view of the story, which has been tamed to present Pinocchio as naughty rather than nasty.

For example, Jiminy Cricket, the much-loved companion

and advisor to Pinocchio in the Disney film, is killed by Pinocchio in the original. In the novel, he is simply called the Talking Cricket and is struck by a hammer thrown by Pinocchio when he tells the wooden boy that a life of idleness will land him in the hospital or prison.

Geppetto has a reputation for being unpleasant before he creates the marionette, but he is put in his place by the demanding Pinocchio, whom he sees as his son. He tries to discipline the wooden boy and to teach him the value of self-lessness. Thus, a peculiar love-hate relationship is established through their codependence. Geppetto needs Pinocchio because he is lonely and needs someone to love. Pinocchio needs Geppetto because he needs food and repair.

Having run away to the theatre, nearly been burned alive and then been swindled by a fox and a cat, Pinocchio is revisited by the Talking Cricket as a ghost. The cricket tries to give Pinocchio guidance but is rebuffed once again when he remarks that the wooden boy will come to grief if he always insists on having things his own way. Pinocchio then embarks on a fantastic and disturbing adventure, where he is pursued by assassins and left for dead, but is then rescued and revived by taking animals and fairies.

In chapter 17, we witness Pinocchio tell three lies, resulting in his nose growing enormously long, so that he becomes trapped in a cottage. His nose is then reduced in size by woodpeckers, enabling Pinocchio to escape and continue on his bizarre journey.

The climax of the Pinocchio story comes when the marionette is transformed into a real boy. After more than two years of struggle, he has finally learned enough lessons in life to know how to behave properly and to show kind-ness. His reward is to become flesh and blood, along with 50 gold coins. This happens after he has rescued Geppetto from incarceration in the stomach of a monstrous shark and they have returned home.

Morals from the Marionette

The allegory in *Pinocchio* is a matter of interpretation, in many respects. The story is so filled with fanciful nonsense that the core theme becomes rather obscured for much of the book. Collodi's main objective seems to be a tale with a moral attached. The moral is that a happy life is more likely to come to those children who behave well and think of others before themselves. Additionally, that children only have themselves to blame for their unhappiness if they fail.

It may seem a little harsh, but that was very much the established view of fate at that time. Succeeding in life was hard work, so it was generally felt that failure resulted from weakness. Darwin had published *On the Origin of Species* in 1859, and people misapprehended his 'survival of the fittest' concept. They dismissed the notion of any disadvantage that came as a consequence of social-cultural environment and nurture, instead putting the onus entirely on the self. The message was black and white: learn to be the fittest you can be and everything else will fall into place because you'll deserve it.

In his early adulthood, Collodi had fought for the Tuscan army in the Italian Wars of Independence, against the Austrian Empire. He had a very keen sense of right and wrong in the world and his forays into literature began with satirical sketches designed to express and disseminate his political views. He was already in his mid-fifties when he began work on *Pinocchio*. He died in his mid-sixties, before the story had had sufficient time to burgeon in popularity and begin to show signs of becoming the classic that we know today.

Pinocchio undoubtedly owes a lot of its mass appeal to Disney; not just for taking the story to a global audience, but also for editing and abridging the story, as well as making the characters more appealing. In the original illustrations, by Italian cartoonist Enrico Mazzanti, Pinocchio is a rather unattractive stick man, with a downward-pointing nose like that of a proboscis monkey. The Disney version is a cute little boy with an upward-pointing, fingerlike nose. Similarly, the Talking Cricket is transformed into Jiminy Cricket, dressed in tails and top hat and with four human limbs instead of an insect's six. Disney took the basic story and used its successful formula to make *Pinocchio* conform to the rest of the portfolio. Some may dislike the 'saccharin treatment' of Disney, but one cannot deny that knew what they were doing.

In chapter 3, when Geppetto is carving Pinocchio from the piece of wood, the nose begins to grow and Geppetto is unable to prevent it from growing, no matter how much he cuts away. In chapter 17, Pinocchio's nose grows because he tells lies. This contrast has led scholars to conclude that Collodi's intention was that Pinocchio's nose actually grows when he is feeling anxious, rather than simply telling lies. So the ubiquitous interpretation of Pinocchio's nose growth as an indicator of untruths is incorrect. It just so happens that telling lies makes Pinocchio feel uneasy, which is why his nose grows. But why quibble over such a detail? The moral that telling lies will show on your face is good advice for children, which is partly why the *Pinocchio* tale has persisted.

The overriding message from *Pinocchio* is that people can change. Pinocchio himself finds compassion and consideration for others after being mistreated by other characters in the story until he realizes what he has run away from was what many children yearn for – a stable and loving home. Geppetto discovers his kindliness by learning to care for someone else apart from himself. Collodi seems to imply that the good in all of us will appear in the right circumstances and that cannot be a bad comment on the human condition in a world where the bad in many people dominates.

PINOCCHIO

CHAPTER 1

How it happened that Mr Cherry, the carpenter, found a piece of wood that laughed and cried like a child

There was once upon a time . . .

'A king!' my little readers will shout together.

No, children, you make a mistake. Once upon a time there was a piece of wood.

It was not the best, but just a common piece of wood, such as is used in stoves and fireplaces to kindle the fire and warm the rooms in winter.

How it happened I cannot tell, but the fact is that one fine day this piece of wood just happened to be there in the shop of an old carpenter whose real name was Mr Antonio, but everyone called him Mr Cherry, because the tip of his nose was always as red and shiny as a ripe cherry.

As soon as Mr Cherry noticed this piece of wood, he was delighted. He rubbed his hands together joyfully and said, 'This has come at exactly the right moment. It is just what I need to make a leg for my little table.'

Then, without hesitating a moment, he took his sharp axe to strip off the bark and the rough part of the wood. But just as he raised the axe for the first blow, he stopped with his arm in the air, for he heard a very tiny voice, begging him gently, 'Don't strike me too hard!'

You can imagine old Mr Cherry's surprise.

He looked round the room to see where the tiny voice had come from, but he saw nobody. He looked under the bench – nobody. He looked in the cupboard which was always shut; but there was nobody. He looked in the basket of chips and sawdust – no one. He opened the door and looked out into the street – no one! What was to be done?

'I see,' he said at last, laughing and scratching his wig, 'I must have imagined that tiny voice. Now let's to work!'

He raised his axe again, and down it went on the piece of wood.

'Oh, you hurt me!' complained the same tiny voice.

This time Mr Cherry was struck all of a heap. His eyes stood out of his head, his mouth was wide open, and his tongue hung out over his chin, as you see on some fountain masks.

As soon as he could speak he said, trembling and stuttering with fright, 'But where did that tiny voice come from that cried "Oh"? There's not a living soul here. Is it possible that this piece of wood has learnt to cry and complain like a baby? I can't believe it. This piece of wood – just look at it! It's nothing but a piece of firewood, like all the others; when you put it on the fire it will make a kettle boil. Well, then? Is someone hidden inside it? If there is, so much the worse for him. I'll attend to him!'

And he took the poor piece of wood in both hands and, without mercy, started to beat it against the wall.

Then he stopped and listened to hear if any tiny voice were complaining this time. He waited two minutes – nothing; five minutes – nothing; ten minutes – and still nothing!

'Now I understand!' he exclaimed, laughing and pulling his wig. 'I must have imagined that tiny voice that said "Oh!" I'd better do my work.' And, because he was very frightened, he began singing to encourage himself.

Meanwhile he put the axe down and, taking his plane, began planing and shaping the piece of wood.

But while the plane went to and fro, he again heard that tiny voice which said, laughing, 'Stop! you're tickling me!'

This time, poor Mr Cherry dropped as if struck by lightning.

When he opened his eyes, he was sitting on the floor. He was so changed you could hardly have recognized him. Even the end of his nose, which was always red, had turned blue with fright.

CHAPTER 2

Mr Cherry gives the piece of wood to his friend, Geppetto, who plans a marvellous puppet that can dance, and fence, and turn somersaults in the air

At that moment somebody knocked on the door. 'Come in!' said the carpenter; but he was too weak to stand up.

A little, jolly old man came into the shop. His name was Geppetto, but when the boys in the neighbourhood wanted to tease him they called him by his nickname of Polendina, because of his yellow wig which looked very like a dish of polenta.

Geppetto was very short-tempered. Woe betide anybody who called him Polendina! He simply went wild, and no one could do anything with him.

'Good morning, Mr Antonio,' said Geppetto. 'What are you doing down there?'

'I am teaching the ants how to read.'

'Much good may it do you!'

'What brought you here, Mr Geppetto?'

'My legs. Mr Antonio, I have come to ask you a favour.'

'Here I am, ready to serve you,' answered the carpenter, getting to his knees.

'I had an idea this morning.'

'Let us hear it.'

'I thought I would make a fine wooden puppet – a really fine one, that can dance, fence, and turn somersaults in the air. Then, with this puppet, I could travel round the world, and earn my bit of bread and my glass of wine. What do you think about it?'

'Bravo, Polendina!' cried that same tiny, mysterious voice.

When he heard the name Polendina, Mr Geppetto became so angry that he turned as red as a ripe pepper. He turned to the carpenter, and said in a fury, 'Why do you annoy me?'

'Who is annoying you?'

'You called me Polendina!'

'No, I didn't!'

'Oh! Perhaps I did it! But I say that it was you.'

'No!'

'Yes!'

'No!'

'Yes!'

And, as they grew more and more excited, from words they came to blows. They seized one another's wigs, and even hit and bit and scratched each other.

At the end of the fight Geppetto's yellow wig was in Mr Antonio's hands, and the carpenter's grey wig between Geppetto's teeth.

'Give me my wig!' said Mr Antonio.

'You give me mine, and let us make a peace treaty!'

So the two little old men, each taking his own wig, shook hands, and promised to be good friends for ever.

'Now, neighbour Geppetto,' said the carpenter, to prove that they were friends again, 'what can I do for you?'

'I would like to have a little piece of wood to make my marionette. Will you give it to me?'

Mr Antonio, pleased as Punch, hurried to his bench, and

took the piece of wood which had frightened him so much. But, just as he was giving it to his friend, it shook so hard that it slipped out of his hands, and struck poor Geppetto's shin.

'Ah! This is a fine way to make me a present, Mr Antonio! You have almost lamed me.'

'Upon my honour, I didn't do it!'

'Oh! So *I* did it then!'

'It's all the fault of this piece of wood –'

'Yes, I know the wood hit me, but you threw it at my legs!'

'I did not throw it at you!'

'That's a lie!'

'Geppetto, don't insult me! If you do, I shall call you Polendina.'

'Blockhead!'

'Polendina!'

'Donkey!'

'Polendina!'

'Ugly monkey!'

'Polendina!'

When he heard himself called Polendina for the third time Geppetto, blind with rage, rushed at the carpenter, and the second fight was worse than the first.

When it was over, Mr Antonio had two more scratches on his nose, and Geppetto two buttons less on his jacket. Honours thus being even, they shook hands again, and vowed to be good friends for ever. Then Geppetto took the piece of wood and, thanking Mr Antonio, went limping home.

CHAPTER 3

*Geppetto goes home and makes his puppet;
he calls him Pinocchio; the puppet gets into
mischief*

Geppetto's little room on the ground floor was lit by a window
under the stairs. His furniture could not have been simpler.
An old chair, a tottering bed, and a broken-down table. At
the back of the room you could see a fireplace, with the fire
lit; but the fire was painted, and over the fire was painted a
kettle boiling merrily, with a cloud of steam that was just like
real steam.

As soon as he arrived home, Geppetto took his tools and
began to make his puppet.

'What shall I call him?' he asked himself. 'I think I shall
call him Pinocchio. That name will bring him good luck. I
once knew a whole family of Pinocchios: there was Pinocchio
the father, and Pinocchia the mother, and Pinocchii the children, and they all got along splendidly. The richest of them
was a beggar.'

Having thought out a name for his puppet, he started
his work with great determination. He made his hair, his
forehead, and his eyes in a very short time.

As soon as the eyes were finished, imagine his bewilderment when he saw them moving and looking at him!

When Geppetto saw those two wooden eyes looking at him, he did not like it at all, and he said angrily, 'Naughty wooden eyes, why are you staring at me?'

But no one answered.

After the eyes, he made the nose; but as soon as it was finished, it began to grow. It grew, and it grew, and in a few minutes' time it was as long as if there was no end to it.

Poor Geppetto worked fast to shorten it; but the more he cut it off, the longer that insolent nose became.

After the nose, he made the mouth; but before he had finished it, it began to laugh and poke fun at him.

'Stop laughing!' said Geppetto; but he might as well have spoken to the wall.

'Stop laughing, I say!' he shouted, menacingly.

The mouth stopped laughing, and stuck out its tongue.

However, as Geppetto did not want to spoil the puppet, he pretended not to see it, and continued his work.

After the mouth, he made the chin, then the neck, the shoulders, the stomach, the arms, and the hands.

As soon as the hands were finished, Geppetto's wig was snatched from his head. He looked up, and what should he see but his yellow wig in the puppet's hands.

'Pinocchio! Give me back my wig at once!'

But Pinocchio, instead of giving back the wig, put it on his own head, and was almost hidden under it.

This cheeky, mocking behaviour made Geppetto feel sadder than ever before in his life. He turned to Pinocchio, and said, 'You scoundrel of a son! You are not even finished, and you already disobey your father! That's bad, my boy – very bad!' And he wiped away a tear.

There were still the legs and feet to make.

When Geppetto had finished the feet, he received a kick on the nose.

'It serves me right,' he said to himself. 'I should have thought of it before. Now it is too late.'

He took the puppet in his hands, and put him down on the floor to see if he could walk; but Pinocchio's legs were stiff, and he did not know how to move them. So Geppetto led him by the hand, and showed him how to put one foot before the other.

When the stiffness went out of his legs, Pinocchio started to walk alone, and run around the room; and finally he slipped through the door into the street and ran away.

Poor old Geppetto ran after him as quickly as he could, but he did not catch him, for the little rascal jumped like a rabbit, and his wooden feet clattered on the pavement, making as much noise as twenty pairs of wooden shoes.

'Catch him! Catch him!' cried Geppetto.

But when the people saw that wooden puppet running as fast as a racehorse, they looked at him in amazement, and then laughed, and laughed, and laughed, until their sides were aching.

At last, by some lucky chance, a policeman came and when he heard the clatter, he thought somebody's horse had run away from its master. So he courageously stood in the middle of the street with his legs apart, in order to stop it, and prevent any more trouble.

From far away, Pinocchio saw the policeman barricading the street, and he decided to run between his legs; but he failed dismally.

The policeman, without moving from his place, picked him up by the nose – that ridiculous, long nose, that seemed made on purpose to be caught by policemen – and returned him to Geppetto, who wanted to pull his ears to punish him for his naughtiness. Imagine what he felt when he could not find any ears! And do you know why? Because he had made him in such a hurry that he had forgotten his ears.

So he took him by the nape of his neck, and as they walked away he said, shaking his head menacingly, 'You just come home, and I'll settle your account when we get there!'

At this threatening remark, Pinocchio threw himself down on the ground, and refused to walk.

A crowd of idle and inquisitive people gathered around him. Some said one thing, some another.

'The poor puppet,' said some of them, 'is right, not wanting to go home! Who knows how horribly that bad Geppetto might beat him?'

And others added, with evil tongues, 'Geppetto *seems* to be a good man, but he is a perfect tyrant with children. If we leave that poor marionette in his hands, he may tear him to pieces.'

In short, so much was said and done that the policeman let Pinocchio go, and decided to take poor Geppetto to prison.

He could not, for the time being, say anything in his own defence, but he cried like a calf and, as they walked towards the prison, he whimpered, 'Wretched son! And to think that I worked so hard to make a fine puppet! But serve me right. I ought to have known what would happen!'

What happened afterwards is almost too much to believe; and I shall tell you about it in the following chapters.

CHAPTER 4

The story of Pinocchio and the talking
cricket in which we see that naughty
children do not like to be corrected by
those who are wiser than they are

Well, I must tell you children, that while poor Geppetto was led to prison through no fault of his own, that rascal Pinocchio, left alone, ran home across the fields as quickly as possible. In his hurry he jumped over high banks, thorn hedges, and ditches full of water, like a kid, or a young hare running away from the hunters.

When he arrived home, he found the door ajar. Pushing it open he went in, and locked it securely after him. Then he threw himself down on the ground with a great sigh of relief.

But the relief did not last long, for he heard someone in the room saying '*Cri-cri-cri!*'

'Who is calling me?' said Pinocchio, frightened.

'It is I.'

Pinocchio turned and saw a big cricket creeping up the wall. 'Tell me, cricket, who are you?'

'I am the talking cricket, and I have lived in this room a hundred years or more.'

'But now this is my room, and you will oblige me by going away at once, without even turning round.'

'I shall not leave,' replied the cricket, 'until I have told you a great truth.'

'Well then, tell me, and be quick about it!'

'Woe to those boys who revolt against their parents, and run away from home. They will never do any good in this world, and sooner or later they will repent bitterly.'

'Sing away, cricket, just as long as you please! But as for me, tomorrow at sunrise I am going to leave; for if I stay here the same will happen to me as happens to other boys: I shall be sent to school, and one way or other, by love or by force, I shall be made to study.'

'You poor fool! Don't you know that, if you spend your time like that, you will grow up to be a great donkey, and everyone will make fun of you?'

'Be quiet, you good for nothing, croaking cricket!' shouted Pinocchio.

But the cricket, who was patient, and a philosopher too, instead of being offended by such impudence, continued in the same tone, 'But if you don't like to go to school, why don't you learn a trade, so that you may at least earn your bread honestly?'

'Do you want me to tell you something?' answered Pinocchio, beginning to lose his patience. 'Of all the trades in the world, there is only one which really attracts me.'

'And what might that be?'

'To eat, drink, sleep, and amuse myself, and to lead a vagabond life from morning to night.'

'Let me tell you,' said the talking cricket, as calm as ever, 'that those who follow that trade finish, nearly always, in a hospital or in prison.'

'Be careful, you cricket of ill omen! If you make me angry, woe betide you!'

'Poor Pinocchio! I am really sorry for you!'

'Why are you sorry for me?'

'Because you are a puppet, and – what is worse – you have a wooden head.'

At these last words Pinocchio lost his temper and, seizing a mallet from the bench, threw it at the cricket.

Perhaps he did not mean to hit him, but unfortunately the mallet struck him right on the head. The poor cricket had scarcely time to cry '*Cri-cri-cri*', and there he was, stretched out stiff, and flattened against the wall.

CHAPTER 5

*Pinocchio is hungry, and he looks for an egg
to make himself an omelette; but just as he
breaks it in the pan the omelette flies
through the window*

It was growing dark, and Pinocchio remembered that he had
eaten nothing all day. There was a painful feeling in his
stomach that closely resembled appetite.

With boys appetite grows fast. In fact, after a few minutes
his appetite became hunger, and in no time he was as hungry
as a wolf. His hunger was unbearable.

Poor Pinocchio hurried to the fireplace where a kettle was
boiling and put out his hand to lift the lid and see what was in
it; but the kettle was only painted on the wall. Imagine his
disappointment! His nose, which was already too long, grew
three inches longer.

He ran about the room, searched in every cupboard and
in every possible place for a little bread – even dry bread. He
would have been grateful for a crust, or a bone left by a dog,
for a fishbone or a cherry stone – in short, for anything he
could chew. But he found nothing, just nothing, absolutely
nothing.

He kept growing hungrier every moment, yet he could
do nothing but yawn. He yawned so tremendously that his

mouth reached his ears; and after he yawned he spattered, and he felt as if he hadn't any stomach left.

At last, in despair, he began to cry, saying, 'The talking cricket was right. I did wrong to revolt against my father and run away from home. If my father were here now, I shouldn't be dying of yawning. Oh, hunger is a dreadful illness!'

Suddenly, in a rubbish heap, he noticed something white and round that looked like an egg. In less than no time he grabbed it. It was really an egg.

To describe his joy would be impossible; you can only imagine it. He feared he might be dreaming. He turned the egg from one hand to the other, and patted it and kissed it as he said, 'Now, how shall I cook it? Shall I make an omelette? No, it would be better to poach it. But perhaps it would be more tasty if I fried it in a pan. Or shall I just boil it in the shell? No, the quickest way would be to poach it. I am just dying to eat it.'

Without further ado, he set a stewing pan over a brazier of red charcoal. Instead of oil or butter, he put some water in it and when the water began to boil – tac! he broke the eggshell and held it over the pan that the contents might drop into it.

But instead of the yolk and white of an egg, a little chicken flew out and, making a polite curtsy, said gaily, 'A thousand thanks, Master Pinocchio, for having spared me the trouble of breaking the shell! Take care of yourself, and give my love to the folks at home. I hope to see you again.'

With that, the chicken spread its wings and, flying through the open window, was soon lost to sight.

The poor puppet stood there as if bewitched, with his eyes fixed, his mouth open, and the broken eggshell in his hands. When he recovered a little from his first bewilderment, he began to cry, and scream, and stamp on the floor in despair; and as he sobbed he said, 'Indeed, the talking cricket was right. If I hadn't run away from home, and if my father were here, I should not now be dying of hunger. Oh, hunger is a dreadful illness!'

His stomach was complaining more than ever and, as he did not know how to quieten it, he decided to go out again into the village, in the hope of meeting some charitable person who would give him some bread.

CHAPTER 6

Pinocchio falls asleep with his feet on the brazier, and, when he wakes up in the morning, finds them burnt off

It was a windy, cold night. The thunder was fierce, and the lightning as violent as though the sky was on fire. A bitter wind whistled angrily, raising clouds of dust and making the trees tremble and groan.

Pinocchio was frightened of thunder, but he was still more hungry than frightened; so he opened the door, and ran as fast as he could to the village, which he soon reached, panting, with his tongue hanging out like a hunting dog's.

But all was dark and quiet. The shops were closed, the doors and windows shut, and there was not even a dog in the street. It seemed a village of the dead.

However Pinocchio, driven by hunger and despair, gave a very long peal at the doorbell of one of the houses, saying to himself, 'This will bring somebody out.'

And indeed, a little old man with a nightcap on his head came to the window, and shouted angrily, 'What do you want at this hour?'

'Will you be so kind as to give me some bread?'

'Wait! I'll be back at once!' said the old man, believing that he had to do with one of those street urchins who amuse themselves at night by ringing doorbells, and rousing good people who are sleeping peacefully.

In half a minute the window was opened, and the same voice called Pinocchio, 'Stand under the window, and hold out your hand!'

Pinocchio held out his hands, and a great kettle of water poured down on him, drenching him from head to foot, as if he had been a pot of dry geraniums.

He went home wet as a rag and exhausted with fatigue and hunger. He had no strength to stand, and so he sat down, and put his wet, muddy feet on the brazier full of burning coal.

Then he fell asleep, and while he was asleep his feet, which were wooden, caught fire, and slowly burned away to cinders.

Pinocchio slept and snored, as though his feet belonged to someone else. At last, at daybreak, he was awakened by someone rapping on the door.

'Who is it?' he called, yawning, and rubbing his eyes.

'It is I!' answered a voice.

And it was the voice of Geppetto.

CHAPTER 7

*Geppetto comes home, and gives Pinocchio
the breakfast that the poor man had brought
for himself*

Poor Pinocchio's eyes were still half closed, and he had
not noticed that his feet were burnt off. Thus, when he
heard his father's voice, he tumbled down from his stool
to run and open the door; but, after staggering a couple
of times, he fell his full length on the floor, making a
noise as of a whole bag of wooden ladles falling from the
fifth storey.

'Open the door!' cried Geppetto from the street.

'I can't, Daddy,' answered the marionette, crying, and
rolling over and over on the floor.

'Why not?'

'Because somebody has eaten my feet!'

'And who has eaten them?'

'The cat,' said Pinocchio, seeing the cat who was just
then playing with some shavings with his forepaws.

'Open the door, I tell you!' Geppetto cried again. 'If you
don't, I'll give you the cat-o'-nine-tails when I get in!'

'Believe me, I can't stand up. Oh, poor me! Poor me! I
shall have to walk on my knees for the rest of my life!'

Geppetto, thinking that all this complaint was just

another of Pinocchio's tricks, decided to end it for good. He climbed up the wall, and got in at the window.

At first he was angry, and scolded him; but, when he saw his own Pinocchio lying on the floor, and really without feet, his anger vanished.

He took him in his arms, kissed and caressed him, spoke many affectionate words and, with tears on his cheeks, he said, sobbing, 'My dear little Pinocchio, how did you burn your feet?'

'I don't know, Daddy. But believe me, it has been a horrid night. I shall never forget it as long as I live. It thundered and lightninged, and I was very hungry, and the talking cricket said, "It serves you right; you have been wicked and you deserve it!" And I said, "Be careful, cricket!" And he said, "You are a puppet, and you have a wooden head!" And I threw the hammer at him, and he died; but it was his fault, for I didn't want to kill him. And the proof of that is that I put the pan on the brazier, but the chicken flew away and said, "Good-bye, I shall see you again. Give my love to the folks!" And I got more and more hungry; and for that reason the little old man with the nightcap opened the window, and said, "Stand under the window and hold up your hat!" And I got a kettleful of water on my head. It isn't a disgrace to ask for a bit of bread, is it? I ran back home as quick as I could; and because I was so very hungry, I put my feet on the brazier to dry them. And then you came home, and I felt that my feet were burnt off, and I'm still so hungry, but I have no more feet! Boo-hoo-hoo!' And poor Pinocchio began to cry and scream so loudly that he could have been heard five miles away.

Geppetto had only understood one thing of all this jumble of words – that Pinocchio was dying of hunger.

He took three pears out of his pocket, and said, giving them to him, 'These three pears were for my breakfast, but I willingly give them to you. Eat them, and may they do you good!'

'If you want me to eat them, kindly peel them for me.'

'Peel them for you?' cried Geppetto, astonished. 'I would never have thought, my lad, that you were so refined and fastidious. That's too bad! We should get used, from childhood, to eating everything, and liking it; for one never knows what might happen in this curious world.'

'That's all very well,' retorted Pinocchio, 'but I'll never eat fruit that isn't peeled. I can't stand skins.'

So that patient, kind Geppetto took a knife and peeled the three pears, putting all the peelings on the corner of the table.

When Pinocchio had eaten the first pear in two mouthfuls, he was about to throw away the core, but Geppetto stopped him.

'Don't throw it away! There might be some use for it.'

'Can you imagine I shall ever eat the core?' cried Pinocchio, turning on him in a rage.

'Who knows! This is a curious world,' replied Geppetto, calmly.

So the three cores, instead of being thrown out of the window, were placed on the corner of the table together with the parings.

When he had eaten, or rather devoured the three pears, Pinocchio yawned, and then began to whimper, 'I'm still hungry.'

'But, my son, I have nothing more to give you.'

'Nothing? Nothing at all?'

'Only the peelings and cores you left.'

'All right!' said Pinocchio. 'If there's really nothing else, I might eat some peelings.'

And he began promptly. At first he made faces; but, one after another, he quickly ate all the peelings; and after them the cores. And when he had eaten everything, he clapped his stomach and said cheerfully, 'Now I feel better!'

'You see,' said Geppetto, 'I was right when I said you should not be so refined and fastidious about your food. My dear boy, we never know what might happen to us. This is a curious world.'

CHAPTER 8

Geppetto makes Pinocchio new feet, and sells his own coat to buy him a primer

As soon as the marionette had satisfied his hunger, he began to cry and grumble because he wanted new feet.

But Geppetto, in order to punish him for all his naughtiness, let him cry and complain for half a day. Then he said, 'Why should I make you new feet? So that you may escape from home again?'

'I promise,' said the marionette, sobbing, 'that from now on I'll be good.'

'All children, when they want something, tell the same story,' replied Geppetto.

'I promise to go to school, and study, and do my best as a good boy should –'

'All children, when they want something, say the same thing.'

'But I'm not like other children! I'm better than all of them, and I always tell the truth. I promise you, daddy, that I shall learn a trade, and be the staff and comfort of your old age.'

Geppetto tried to look very severe; but his eyes were full of tears, and his heart was full of sadness when he saw his poor Pinocchio in such a dreadful state. He did not say another word, but, taking his tools and two little pieces of seasoned wood, he set to work as hard as he could.

In less than an hour the feet were ready – two well-shaped, nimble swift little feet that might have been carved by a great artist.

Then Geppetto said to Pinocchio, 'Shut your eyes and go to sleep.'

Pinocchio shut his eyes, and pretended to be asleep. And while he did so Geppetto, with some glue melted in an eggshell, fastened the feet in place; and he did it so neatly that no one could even see where they were joined together. As soon as Pinocchio discovered he had his feet again, he jumped down from the table where he was lying and began to gambol and dance around the room, nearly mad with joy.

'Now, to prove to you how grateful I am,' said Pinocchio to his father, 'I want to go to school at once.'

'What a good boy!'

'But if I'm going to school, I must have some clothes.'

Geppetto, who was poor and had not a farthing in his pocket, made Pinocchio a suit out of flowered paper, a pair of shoes out of bark from a tree, and a cap out of bread.

Pinocchio ran to look at himself in a basin of water; and he was so pleased with himself that he said, as he strutted about, 'I look exactly like a gentleman!'

'Yes, indeed,' answered Geppetto, 'but remember, it is not fine clothes that make a gentleman, but clean clothes.'

'By the way, speaking of school,' added Pinocchio, 'there's still something I must have – the most necessary of all.'

'And that is . . .?'

'I have no primer.'

'That's right. But how shall I get one?'

'That's easy! Go to the bookseller and buy one.'

'And the money?'

'I haven't any.'

'Neither have I,' added the good old man, sadly.

Pinocchio, although he was usually very cheerful, became sad, too; for poverty, when it is real poverty, destroys all joy, even in children.

'Wait,' Geppetto cried suddenly and, jumping up, he put on his old coat, full of holes and patches, and ran out of the shop.

In a little while he was back again, with a primer in his hand for Pinocchio. But the poor man was in his shirt-sleeves, and it was snowing outside.

'Where is your coat, Daddy?'

'I have sold it.'

'Why did you sell it?'

'Because it made me too warm.'

Pinocchio understood this answer instantly; and he was so overcome by the feelings of his good heart, that he threw his arms around Geppetto's neck and kissed him again and again.

CHAPTER 9

*Pinocchio sells his primer that he may go
and see the marionettes*

When it stopped snowing, Pinocchio started for school with
his fine new primer under his arm. On the way, he never
stopped imagining all sorts of fine plans, and he built a thousand
castles in the air, each one more beautiful than the other.

He began by saying to himself, 'At school today I shall
learn to read in no time; tomorrow I shall learn to write, and
the day after tomorrow I shall learn all the figures. Then I
shall be clever enough to earn lots of money; and with the
very first money I get I shall buy my father the nicest, new,
cloth coat. But why cloth? It shall be made of gold and silver,
with diamond buttons. That poor man really deserves it; for,
that I should be a learned man, he sold his coat to buy me a
book – in this cold weather, too! Only fathers can make such
sacrifices.'

While he was saying this more and more excitedly, he
thought he heard music in the distance that sounded like fife
and drum: *fi-fi-fi . . . zum, zum, zum, zum.*

He stopped and listened. The sounds came from the end
of the street that crossed the one which led to school, at the
end of the little village near the sea.

'What can the music be? What a pity I have to go to

school! Otherwise . . .' He hesitated, deciding whether to go to school or listen to the fifes.

'Today I shall listen to the fifes, and tomorrow I shall go to school,' this naughty boy said finally, shrugging his shoulders.

No sooner said than done. He ran, and the farther he ran the more distinctly he heard the tune of the fifes and the beating of the big drum: *fi-fi-fi, fi-fi-fi . . . zum, zum, zum*.

At last he came to a little square full of people who were gathered around a great building of boards and cloth, painted in all colours of the rainbow.

'What is that big building?' Pinocchio asked a boy who seemed to live there.

'Read the poster – it is all written there – and then you'll know.'

'I'd gladly read it, but I don't know how to read today.'

'Bravo, nincompoop! I'll read it for you. Know, then, that on that big poster, in fiery red letters, is written: GREAT PUPPET SHOW.'

'Is it long since the play began?'

'It's just beginning now.'

'How much does it cost to go in?'

'Twopence.'

Pinocchio was in such a fever of curiosity that he lost his self-control and without any shame, he said to the little boy, 'Will you lend me twopence until tomorrow?'

'I'd simply love to,' said the boy, laughing at him, 'but I can't today.'

'I shall sell you my jacket for twopence,' said the puppet.

'What could I do with a jacket of flowered paper? If it should rain and got wet, I couldn't take it off.'

'Will you buy my shoes?'

'They're only good for lighting a fire.'

'What will you give me for my cap?'

'That would be a fine bargain! A cap made of bread! The mice might eat it right off my head!'

Pinocchio was sitting on horns. He was almost ready to make one more offer, but he had not the courage. He hesitated, but at last he said, 'Will you buy this new primer for twopence?'

'I am only a boy, and I do not buy anything from other boys,' said the other, having more sense than the puppet.

'I'll give you twopence for the primer,' cried an old-clothes dealer who had overheard the conversation.

The book was sold at once. And to think that poor Geppetto stayed at home shivering in his shirt-sleeves, because he had to sell his coat to buy that primer for his son!

CHAPTER 10

The puppets recognize Pinocchio as one of them, and are pleased to see him, but Fireeater, the Showman, appears in the midst of their joy, and Pinocchio almost comes to a bad end

When Pinocchio entered the puppet show, he nearly caused a revolution. You must know that the curtain was up, and they had just started the play.

Harlequin and Punchinello were on the stage, quarrelling as usual, threatening every moment to come to blows.

The audience paid the closest attention, and were laughing until they were sore to see those two puppets quarrelling and gesticulating and calling each other names, just as if they were truly two reasoning beings, two real persons.

But all at once Harlequin stopped and, turning to the public, pointed to the pit of the theatre, and shouted dramatically:

'Heavens above! Am I awake, or am I dreaming? That must be Pinocchio there!'

'Yes, it's indeed Pinocchio!' cried Punchinello.

'It is indeed!' exclaimed Miss Rosy, peeping from the back of the stage.

'Here's Pinocchio! Here's Pinocchio!' shouted all the

puppets in chorus, running to the stage from every wing. 'Here's Pinocchio! Here's our brother Pinocchio! Hurrah for Pinocchio!'

'Come up here to me, Pinocchio!' cried Harlequin. 'Come and throw yourself into the arms of your wooden brothers!'

At this affectionate invitation, Pinocchio made one jump from the back of the pit to the front seats. Another jump, and he landed on the head of the orchestra leader; and from there he jumped to the stage.

It is impossible to describe the hugging and kissing that followed, the friendly pinches, the brotherly taps that Pinocchio received from the actors and actresses of that puppet company.

It was a very spectacular sight, but the audience, when they saw that the play had stopped, grew impatient and began shouting, 'The play! We want the play! Go on with the play!'

However, their breath was wasted, for the puppets, instead of continuing the play, redoubled their noise and, placing Pinocchio on their shoulders, carried him in triumph before the footlights.

Suddenly the Showman appeared. He was very tall, and so ugly that he frightened anyone who looked at him. His beard was like black ink, and it was so long that it reached the ground. Believe me, he stepped on it when he walked. His mouth was as big as an oven, his eyes were like two burning red lanterns, and he was constantly cracking a great whip made of serpents and foxes' tails, twisted together.

When the Showman appeared so unexpectedly, everybody was speechless. No one breathed. You could have heard a fly in the air. Even the poor puppets, male and female, trembled like so many leaves.

'Why have you come here to disturb my theatre?' he asked Pinocchio, in a voice like that of a spook with a bad cold in his head.

'Believe me, Your Honour, it was not my fault.'

'Not another word! We shall settle our accounts tonight.'

As soon as the show was over, the Showman went into the kitchen, where the whole sheep, which he was preparing for his supper, was roasting on the slowly turning spit.

When he saw that there was not enough wood to finish roasting it, he called Harlequin and Punchinello and said, 'Bring me in Pinocchio! You will find him hanging on a nail. He is made of nice, dry wood, and I am sure he will make a good fire for my roast.'

At first Harlequin and Punchinello hesitated; but, when the Showman glanced at them menacingly, they obeyed. In a few moments they returned to the kitchen carrying poor Pinocchio, who was wriggling like an eel out of water, and shouting desperately,

'O Daddy, O Daddy, save me! I don't want to die. I don't want to die!'

CHAPTER 11

*Fire-eater sneezes and pardons Pinocchio,
who later saves the life of his friend
Harlequin*

Fire-eater, for that was the Showman's name, looked a horrid man, there can be no doubt about it, particularly with his black beard hanging down like an apron covering his chest and legs. Yet at heart, he was really not so bad. When he saw poor Pinocchio struggling and crying, 'I don't want to die! I don't want to die!' he felt sorry for him and, although he tried not to, at last he could not help it and sneezed violently.

Harlequin, who had been sad and downhearted, and looking like a weeping willow, when he heard that sneeze, became cheerful, and bending towards Pinocchio, whispered, 'Good news, brother! The Showman has sneezed. That's a sign that he's pitying you, and you are saved.'

For you must know that, whilst other men weep, or at least pretend to wipe their eyes, when they pity somebody, whenever Fire-eater really pitied anyone, he had the habit of sneezing.

After the Showman had sneezed, he continued speaking gruffly, and shouted at Pinocchio, 'Can't you stop crying? It gives me a nasty feeling in my stomach. I feel such a pain that . . . that . . . Atchoo! Atchoo!' – and this time he sneezed twice.

'God bless you!' said Pinocchio.

'Thank you. And your father and mother, are they alive?' asked Fire-eater.

'My father is, but I never knew my mother.'

'Who knows how sorry your old father would be if I threw you on the fire! Poor old man! I pity him. A-tchoo! A-tchoo! A-tchoo!' – and he sneezed three times.

'Bless you!' cried Pinocchio.

'Thank you. But on the other hand, you must be sorry for me, too, because, as you see, I haven't enough wood to finish roasting my mutton – and believe me, you certainly would have been very useful. But now I have spared you, and I must not complain. Instead of you, I shall burn some puppet of my company under the spit. Come on, gendarmes!'

Two wooden gendarmes appeared immediately at this command. They were very tall, and very thin. They wore helmets, and carried drawn swords in their hands.

The Showman ordered them hoarsely, 'Take that Harlequin, bind him strongly and throw him on the fire. My mutton must be well roasted!'

Imagine poor Harlequin! He was so frightened that his legs bent under him, and he fell on his face.

At this heart-breaking sight, Pinocchio knelt down at the Showman's feet and, weeping, he soused with tears the whole length of his long beard. Then he pleaded, 'Have mercy, Sir Fire-eater!'

'There are no sirs here!' replied the Showman, sternly.

'Have mercy, cavalier!'

'There are no cavaliers here!'

'Have mercy, commander!'

'There are no commanders here!'

'Have mercy, Your Excellency!'

When he heard himself called Your Excellency, the Showman smiled with his lips and, suddenly growing kind and calmer, asked Pinocchio, 'Well, what can I do for you?'

'I implore you to pardon poor Harlequin!'

'It cannot be done. As I pardoned you, I must put him on the fire, for my mutton must be well roasted.'

'In that case,' cried Pinocchio, rising and throwing away his cap of bread, 'in that case, I know my duty. Forward, gendarmes! Bind me and throw me in the fire! It is not just that poor Harlequin, my truest friend, should die for me.'

These words, shouted in a loud, heroic voice, caused all the marionettes present to weep. Even the gendarmes, although made of wood, cried like newborn babies.

At first Fire-eater remained as hard and cold as ice: slowly he began to melt, and to sneeze. When he had sneezed four or five times, he opened his arms affectionately to Pinocchio, saying, 'You are a good, brave boy! Come here, and give me a kiss.'

Pinocchio ran quickly and, climbing up the Showman's beard like a squirrel, gave him a loud kiss on the tip of his nose.

'And is my life spared?' asked poor Harlequin, in a trembling voice that could hardly be heard.

'Your life is spared,' replied Fire-eater. Then he added, shaking his head, 'Very well, then! This evening I must eat my mutton half done; but another time, woe to him who . . .!'

When they knew that their brothers were pardoned, all the puppets ran back to the stage, lit all the lights as for a festive performance, and began to jump and dance. They were still dancing at dawn.

CHAPTER 12

Fire-eater gives Pinocchio five pieces of gold to take to his father Geppetto: but Pinocchio is deceived by the fox and the cat, and goes away with them

The next day Fire-eater called Pinocchio aside and asked him, 'What is your father's name?'

'Geppetto.'

'And what is his trade?'

'That of a very poor man.'

'Does he earn very much?'

'He earns as much as he needs for never having a farthing in his pocket. Just imagine, in order to buy a primer for my schooling, he had to sell his only coat: a coat that was so full of holes and patches that it was shameful.'

'Poor fellow! I am almost sorry for him. Here are five gold pieces. Hurry up and give them to him, with my compliments.'

As you can well imagine, Pinocchio thanked the Showman a thousand times. One after another he embraced all the puppets of the company, even the gendarmes; then, almost beside himself with joy, he set out for home.

But before he had gone far he met a fox who was lame in one foot, and a cat who was blind in both eyes, getting along as best they could, like good companions in misfortune. The fox, who was lame, was leaning on the cat: and the cat, who was blind, was guided by the fox.

'Good morning, Pinocchio,' said the fox, approaching politely.

'How do you know my name?' asked the puppet.

'I know your father well.'

'Where did you see him?'

'I saw him yesterday, at the gate of his house.'

'And what was he doing?'

'He was in his shirt-sleeves, and trembling with cold.'

'Poor Daddy! But never mind! From now on, he will shiver no more.'

'Why not?'

'Because I am now a rich man.'

'You? A rich man?' said the fox. And he began to laugh rudely and scornfully.

The cat laughed, too; but to hide it, she stroked her whiskers with her forepaws.

'There's nothing to laugh at,' cried Pinocchio angrily. 'I'm really sorry if what I say whets your appetite, but as you can see, there – if you understand such things – are five gold pieces.' And he showed the money that Fire-eater had given him.

At the fascinating ringing of gold, the fox made an involuntary movement with the paw that seemed lame, and the cat opened wide her two blind eyes, but shut them again so quickly that Pinocchio could not notice.

'And now,' asked the fox, 'what are you going to do with the money?'

'First of all,' answered the marionette, 'I shall buy a beautiful new coat for my father – a coat made of gold and silver, and with diamond buttons. Then I will buy myself a primer.'

'For yourself?'

'Of course; for I mean to go to school and study hard.'

'Look at me,' said the fox. 'It is because of my foolish passion for study that I lost the use of my leg.'

'And look at me,' said the cat. 'Because of *my* foolish passion for study, I lost the sight of both my eyes.'

At that very moment, a white blackbird that was sitting on a hedge by the road sang its usual song, and said, 'Pinocchio, don't listen to the advice of evil companions. If you do, you'll regret it.'

Poor blackbird, if only he had not said it! The cat, with a great leap, jumped upon him and, without giving him time to say 'oh', swallowed him in a mouthful, feathers and all.

Having devoured him she wiped her mouth, shut her eyes and shammed blindness as before.

'Poor blackbird!' said Pinocchio. 'Why did you treat him so?'

'I did it to give him a lesson. He will learn not to be meddlesome again, when other people are talking.'

They had gone nearly half-way towards Pinocchio's home, when the fox suddenly stopped and said, 'Would you like to double your fortune?'

'How do you mean?'

'Would you like to multiply those five miserable gold pieces into a hundred, a thousand, two thousand times?'

'Who wouldn't! But how?'

'That's very easy. But instead of going home, you must come with us.'

'And where are you going?'

'We are going to Dupeland.'

Pinocchio thought for a moment, and then said resolutely, 'No, I'm not going. I'm nearly at home, and I want to go to my father, who is waiting for me. Who knows how much he suffered because I didn't come home? I know I have been a very bad boy, and that the talking cricket was right when he said, "Disobedient children never do any good in this world." I have learnt it at my expense, for I have suffered many misfortunes! And last night, in Fire-eater's house, I was nearly . . . Oh, even to think of it, makes me shiver!'

'Well, then,' said the fox, 'so you really want to go home? Run along, then, and so much the worse for you!'

'So much the worse for you!' repeated the cat.

'Think well, Pinocchio, because you're losing a fortune!'

'A fortune!' repeated the cat.

'Your five gold pieces might become two thousand in one day!'

'Two thousand!' repeated the cat.

'But how could they possibly become so many?' demanded Pinocchio, opening his mouth wide in astonishment.

'I'll explain it to you right now,' said the fox.

'You must know that in Dupeland there is a sacred field called the Field of Miracles. You dig a little hole in this field, and you put in it, let's say, a gold piece. Then you cover it with earth, water it from the spring with two buckets of water, sprinkle two pinches of salt over it, and go quietly to bed. During the night the gold pieces will grow and blossom; and the next morning, when you get up and go back to the field, what do you find? You find a marvellous tree, laden with as many gold pieces as an ear of corn has grains at harvest-time.'

'Suppose,' said Pinocchio, more bewildered than ever, 'that I buried my five gold pieces in that field, how many should I find there the next morning?'

'That's very easy to tell,' replied the fox. 'It's a problem that can be solved on your fingers. Suppose every gold piece yields five hundred gold pieces; multiply five hundred by five, and the next morning you will find in your pocket two thousand five hundred shining gold pieces.'

'Oh, wonderful!' shouted Pinocchio, dancing for joy. 'When I have collected these gold pieces, I shall keep two thousand for myself, and I shall make a present of the other five hundred to both of you.'

'A present – to us?' exclaimed the fox, as if offended. 'God forbid!'

'God forbid!' repeated the cat.

'We do not work for gain,' said the fox. 'We do everything for other people.'

'For other people,' echoed the cat.

'What good people!' thought Pinocchio. And, instantly forgetting his father, the new coat, the primer, and all his good resolutions, he said to the fox and the cat, 'Well, let's start! I shall come with you.'

CHAPTER 13

The Red Crab Inn

They walked, and walked, and walked, and finally towards evening, tired out, they arrived at the Red Crab Inn.

'Let us stop here a little while,' said the Fox, 'that we may eat a bite, and rest a few hours. At midnight we must go on again, so that we can reach the Field of Miracles early tomorrow morning.'

They entered the inn, and sat down at a table, but none of them had any appetite.

The poor cat had a bad indigestion, and could eat no more than thirty-five mullet with tomato sauce, and four helpings of tripe with Parmesan cheese; and, because she thought the tripe was not well seasoned, she asked three times for the butter and grated cheese.

The fox, too, would gladly have nibbled at something, but since the doctor had put him on a strict diet, he had to be content with a hare in sweet-savoury sauce, garnished with fat spring chickens and young pullets. After the hare, he ordered a special dish composed of partridges, rabbits, frogs, lizards, and other titbits, but he would not touch anything more. He said he was so disgusted at the sight of food that he could not eat another mouthful.

The one who ate least of all was Pinocchio. He asked

for some nuts and some bread, but he left them all on his plate. The poor child's thoughts were fixed on the Field of Miracles, and he was suffering a mental indigestion of gold pieces.

When they had supped, the fox said to their host, 'Give us two nice rooms – one for Mr Pinocchio, and the other for me and my friend. We shall take a little nap before we leave. Don't forget that, at midnight, we must continue our journey.'

'Yes, sir,' replied the host, winking at the fox and the cat as if to say, 'I understand what you are up to. We know each other.'

As soon as he was in bed, Pinocchio fell asleep, and began to dream. He dreamed that he was in the middle of a field, and the field was full of small trees, the branches of which were laden with gold pieces swinging gently in the breeze, and chattering as if to say, 'Whoever wants us, come and take us!' But just at the most interesting moment – that is, when Pinocchio stretched out his hand to pick a handful and put them in his pocket – he was suddenly awakened by three violent knocks on the door.

It was the innkeeper, who came to tell him that it was midnight.

'Are my companions ready?' asked Pinocchio.

'Ready! They left two hours ago.'

'Why were they in such a hurry?'

'Because the cat received a message that her eldest son was very sick with chilblains, and not expected to live.'

'Did they pay for our supper?'

'What an idea! They were far too well-mannered to offer such an insult to a gentleman like you.'

'That's too bad! Such an insult would have been a great pleasure!' said Pinocchio, scratching his head. Then he inquired, 'And where did those good friends of mine say they would wait for me?'

'In the Field of Miracles, tomorrow morning, at sunrise.'

Pinocchio paid for his supper, and that of his friends, with a gold piece, and left. It was so dark that he had to grope his way, and it was impossible to see as far as his hand before his face. In the country round him, not a leaf stirred. Only a few night birds, flying across the road from one hedge to the other, brushed Pinocchio's nose with their wings, frightening him so that he jumped back, crying, 'Who goes there?'

An echo answered from the distant hills, 'Who goes there? Who goes there? Who goes there?'

As he walked on he saw a little creature on the trunk of a tree, which shone with a pale faint light, like a night lamp with a china shade.

'Who are you?' asked Pinocchio.

'I am the ghost of the talking cricket,' was the reply, in a low, low voice, so faint that it seemed to come from another world.

'What do you want from me?' said the marionette.

'I want to give you some advice. Go back home, and carry the four gold pieces you have left to your poor father, who is weeping and longing for you.'

'Tomorrow my father will be a rich gentleman, for these four gold pieces will have become two thousand.'

'My boy, never trust people who promise to make you rich in a day. They are generally crazy swindlers. Listen to me, and go back home.'

'No, on the contrary, I am going forward.'

'It is very late.'

'I am going forward.'

'The night is dark.'

'I am going forward.'

'It's a dangerous road . . .'

'I am going forward.'

'Remember that children who do as they please and want to have their own way, are sorry for it sooner or later.'

'That's an old story. Good night, cricket!'

'Good night, Pinocchio. May Heaven preserve you from dangers and assassins!'

With these words, the talking cricket disappeared as suddenly as when you blow out a candle; and the path was darker than before.

CHAPTER 14

Pinocchio does not listen to the good advice of the talking cricket, and meets the assassins

'Really,' said Pinocchio to himself, as he continued his journey, 'how unfortunate we poor boys are! Everybody scolds us, everybody warns us, everybody advises us. When they talk you would think they are all our fathers, or our school-masters – all of them: even the talking cricket. Just imagine – because I would not listen to that tiresome talking cricket, who knows, according to him, how many misfortunes will befall me? I shall even meet some assassins! Fortunately I don't believe, and never have believed, in assassins. I am sure that assassins have been invented by fathers to frighten us, so that we should not dare to go out at night. But supposing I should meet them, on the road, would I be afraid of them? Certainly not! I should walk straight up to them and say, "Mr Assassins, what do you want from me? Just remember that there's no joking with me. You had better be quiet, and go about your business!" If those wretched assassins heard me talking like that, I can just see them running away like the wind. But if, by chance, they didn't run away, I would and that would be the end of it.'

Pinocchio would have continued his musings, but at that moment he thought he heard a rustling of leaves behind him.

Turning quickly, he saw two frightful black figures wrapped in charcoal sacks leaping towards him on tiptoe, like two spectres.

'There they are, for sure!' he said to himself and, not knowing where to hide his gold pieces, he put them in his mouth, under his tongue.

Then he tried to run away; but before he could take the first step, he felt himself seized by his arms, and heard two horrible, cavernous voices cry, 'Your money, or your life!'

Pinocchio not being able to speak, since the money was in his mouth, made a thousand bows and gestures to show those masked fellows, whose eyes were visible only through holes in the sacks, that he was a poor puppet, and hadn't even a counterfeit farthing in his pocket.

'Come, come! Less nonsense, and hand over your money!' the two brigands cried menacingly.

But the puppet made signs with his hands, as if to say, 'I haven't any!'

'Hand over your money, or you are dead!' said the taller of the assassins.

'Dead!' repeated the other.

'And after we have killed you, we shall kill your father, too!'

'Your father, too!' repeated the other.

'No, no, no, not my poor father!' cried Pinocchio in despair. But as he spoke, the gold pieces clinked in his mouth.

'Ah, ha, you rascal! So you hid your money under your tongue! Spit it out, at once!'

Pinocchio did not obey.

'Oh, so you cannot hear what we say? Wait a moment, we'll make you spit it out!'

And one of them seized the puppet by the end of his nose, and the other by his chin, and they pulled without mercy, one up, the other down, to make him open his mouth; but it was no use. Pinocchio's mouth was as tightly closed as if it had been nailed and riveted.

Then the smaller assassin drew a horrid knife, and tried to force it between his lips, like a chisel, but Pinocchio, quick as lightning, bit off his hand and spat it out. Imagine his astonishment when he saw that it was a cat's paw he spat to the ground!

Encouraged by this first victory, using his nails he freed himself from the assassins and, jumping over the hedge by the roadside, fled across the country. The assassins ran after him, like dogs after a hare. The smaller one, who had lost a paw, ran on one leg, though goodness knows how he did it.

After they had run miles and miles, Pinocchio was completely exhausted. Seeing himself lost, he climbed a very tall pine-tree, and seated himself on its highest branch. The assassins tried to climb after him, but half-way up they slipped and fell to the ground, hurting their hands and feet.

Yet they did not give up. They gathered a heap of dry sticks at the foot of the tree, and set fire to it. In less than no time the pine started to burn, and blazed like a candle in the wind. Pinocchio, seeing that the flames were mounting fast, and not wanting to end his life like a roasted pigeon, leaped down from the tree-top, and ran again across the fields and vineyards. The assassins followed him, running close without seeming a bit tired.

It was nearly daybreak, and they were still running, when suddenly Pinocchio found the way barred by a wide, deep ditch full of dirty, coffee-coloured water. What was he to do?

'One, two, three!' cried the puppet and, dashing forward, he jumped over it. The assassins jumped, too; but they had not judged the distance properly, and – Swash! Splash! – they fell right in the middle of the ditch.

Pinocchio heard the splashing of water and, running, he laughed, and shouted, 'A good bath to you, Mr Assassins!'

He was sure that they were drowned, when, turning to look, he saw them both running after him, still wrapped in their sacks, from which the water was dripping as if they were two leaky baskets.

CHAPTER 15

The assassins follow Pinocchio and, having caught him, hang him on a branch of the big oak tree

This time, the puppet thought that the end was near. He was ready to fall to the ground and surrender when he noticed a little house, as white as snow, far away among the dark green trees.

'If I had enough breath to get to that house, perhaps I'd be safe,' he told himself.

Wasting no time, he ran through the wood, with the assassins on his track.

After a desperate race of nearly two hours, he arrived at last, worn out, at the door of the little house.

He knocked, but no one answered.

He knocked again, louder, for he heard the footsteps of the assassins; but all was silent as before.

Seeing that it was useless to knock, he began kicking the door, and beating it with his head. At that, a lovely child opened the window. Her hair was blue, and her face as white as wax; her eyes were closed, and her hands were crossed on her breast.

Without moving her lips she said in a very low voice that seemed to come from another world, 'There is nobody in this house. They are all dead.'

'But at least you should open the door and let me in,' cried Pinocchio, weeping, and entreating her.

'I am dead, too.'

'Dead? Then what are you doing at the window?'

'I am waiting for the bier to come, and take me away.'

As she said this she disappeared, and the window closed itself, silently.

'Oh, beautiful blue-haired child,' cried Pinocchio, 'open the door, for pity's sake! Have mercy on a poor boy pursued by assass –'

But before he could finish, he felt himself seized by the neck, and heard those cruel threatening voices, 'This time you won't escape!'

The puppet, feeling that his end was near, began to tremble, so violently that the joints of his wooden legs creaked, and the gold pieces under his tongue clinked together.

'Now, then,' demanded the assassins, 'will you open your mouth, or will you not? You won't answer, eh? Well, leave it to us. We'll open it for you this time!'

And, drawing two great knives as sharp as razors – Slash! they stabbed him savagely.

Luckily the puppet was made of the hardest wood, and the knives broke into a thousand pieces. Only the handles remained in the assassins' hands, who stood staring at each other.

'Now I see,' said one of them, 'he must be hung. Let us hang him!'

'Let us hang him!' repeated the other.

No sooner said than done. They bound his arms behind his back and, putting a running noose around his throat, they tied him to a branch of a big oak tree.

Then they sat down on the grass, and waited for his last kick; but after three hours, the puppet's eyes were still wide open, and he was kicking stronger than ever.

Losing their patience, and tired of waiting, they turned

to Pinocchio, and said with a sneering voice, 'Good-bye, until tomorrow, when we shall be back. And let's hope you'll be so polite as to see that we find you very dead, and your mouth wide open!' Then they left.

Meanwhile, a stormy north wind had begun to blow, and it raged, and whistled, and blew the poor puppet back and forth as fast as a bell-clapper on a wedding-day. It hurt him dreadfully, and the running noose tightened around his throat so that he could not breathe.

Little by little his eyes grew dim, and, although he felt that death was near, still he hoped that some kind person might come and save him. He waited and waited, but nobody came – absolutely nobody.

Then he remembered his poor father, and he stammered, half dead as he was, 'O Daddy! If only you were here!'

He could say no more. He closed his eyes, opened his mouth, stretched out his legs, shuddered all over, and became stiff.

CHAPTER 16

*The beautiful blue-haired child saves the
puppet; she puts him in bed, and calls three
doctors to know whether he is alive or dead*

While poor Pinocchio, hung on a branch of the big oak tree,
seemed more dead than alive, the beautiful child with blue
hair looked out of the window again. She felt very sorry for
the unfortunate puppet who, hanging by his neck, was
dancing to the music of the cold north wind. She clapped
her hands three times, faintly.

At this signal there was a rustling as of flapping wings,
and a large falcon flew to the window-sill.

'What are your orders, beautiful fairy?' asked the falcon,
lowering his beak in reverence – for you must know that the
child with blue hair was no other than a good-hearted fairy,
who had lived in that wood for more than a thousand years.

'Do you see that puppet hanging on a branch of the big
oak?'

'I see him.'

'Very well. Fly there quickly; break the knot that holds
him, with your strong beak, and lay him gently on the grass
at the foot of the tree.'

The falcon flew away, and in two minutes he returned
saying, 'I obeyed your order.'

'How did you find him?'

'He seems to be dead, but he cannot be quite dead, for as soon as I loosened the running noose that strangled his neck, he murmured, "Now I feel better!"'

The fairy clapped her hands twice, and a magnificent poodle appeared, walking upright on his hind legs, as if he were a man. The poodle was dressed like a coachman in his Sunday best. He had a three-cornered hat trimmed with gold, a white curly wig reaching his shoulders, a chocolate-coloured waistcoat with diamond buttons and two large pockets for the bones his mistress gave him at dinner, a pair of breeches of crimson velvet, silk stockings, low boots, and a kind of umbrella case, made of blue satin, to put his tail in when it was raining.

'Be quick, Medoro!' said the fairy. 'Get out my finest carriage from my coach house, and drive to the wood. When you come to the big oak, you will find a poor puppet lying, half dead, on the grass. Take him up gently, put him on the cushions, and bring him to me. Do you understand?'

The poodle, to show that he understood, wagged the blue satin case he carried behind three or four times, and off he ran.

In a few minutes a beautiful carriage was driven out of the coach house. It was the colour of fresh air, and the cushions were padded with canary feathers and lined with whipped cream and custard, with sweet biscuits. It was drawn by a hundred pairs of white mice, and the poodle sitting on the box, cracked his whip like a driver afraid of being late.

In less than a quarter of an hour the carriage was back again. The fairy, who was waiting at the door, took the poor puppet in her arms, carried him to a little room whose walls were mother-of-pearl, and sent at once for the most famous doctors in the neighbourhood.

The doctors came in a hurry, one after another. They were a crow, an owl, and a talking cricket.

'Gentlemen, I should like you to tell me,' said the fairy, as the doctors stood around Pinocchio's bed, 'I should like you gentlemen to tell me if this unfortunate puppet is dead or alive.'

The crow came forward first, and felt Pinocchio's pulse; then he felt his nose, and finally his little toe. Having examined them carefully he solemnly declared, 'It is my opinion that this puppet is quite dead; but if, unfortunately, he is not dead, then that would be a sure sign that he is still alive.'

'I regret very much,' said the owl, 'to contradict the crow, my illustrious friend and colleague, but according to my opinion this puppet is still alive; but if, unfortunately, he is not alive, then that would be a sign that he is really dead.'

'And have you nothing to say?' inquired the fairy, turning to the talking cricket.

'I think that when a prudent physician does not know what to say, the wisest thing he can do is to remain silent. For the rest, this puppet's face is not new to me; I have seen him before.'

Pinocchio, who until that moment had seemed as lifeless as a real piece of wood, started to shudder, shaking the whole bed.

'That puppet there,' continued the talking cricket, 'is a perfect rogue . . .'

Pinocchio opened his eyes, but closed them again quickly.

'He is a rogue, a good-for-nothing, a vagabond . . .'

Pinocchio hid his face beneath the sheet.

'That puppet is a disobedient son, who will make his poor old father die of a broken heart!'

Just then a smothered sobbing and crying could be heard in the room. Imagine everybody's surprise when, lifting up the sheet a little, they saw that Pinocchio was crying.

CARLO COLLODI

'When a dead boy weeps, it's a sign that he is on the way to recovery,' said the crow, solemnly.

'I am sorry to contradict my illustrious friend and colleague,' said the owl, 'but according to my opinion the sign indicates that he does not want to die.'

CHAPTER 17

Pinocchio eats the sugar, but won't take the medicine; however, when he sees the gravediggers coming to carry him away, he takes it; then he tells a lie, and his nose grows longer as punishment

As soon as the three doctors had left the room, the fairy came to Pinocchio. She touched his forehead with her hand, and felt that he had a dangerous fever.

Thereupon she dissolved some white powder in half a glass of water and, holding it to his lips, said lovingly, 'Drink this, and in a few days you will be better.'

Pinocchio looked at the glass, made a sour face, and asked in a complaining voice, 'Is it sweet, or bitter?'

'It is bitter, but it will do you good.'

'If it's bitter I won't drink it.'

'Listen to me, and drink it!'

'I don't like anything bitter.'

'If you drink it, I shall give you a lump of sugar, to take the taste out of your mouth.'

'Where is the lump of sugar?'

'Here it is,' said the fairy, taking one out of a golden sugar basin.

'First I want the lump of sugar, and then I'll drink the horrid bitter water.'

'You promise to drink it?'

'Yes.'

The fairy gave him the sugar, and Pinocchio crunched and swallowed it in a second, saying as he licked his lips, 'It would be fine if sugar were medicine. I'd take it every day.'

'Now keep your promise, and drink these few drops of water. They will bring back your health.'

Pinocchio took the glass in his hand unwillingly. He brought it to his nose, and held it to his lips, then again to his nose, and at last he said, 'It's too bitter! It's too bitter! I can't drink it.'

'How can you tell, when you haven't even tasted it!'

'Oh, I know it is! I know it from its smell. Give me another lump of sugar, and then I'll drink it.'

So the fairy, with all the patience of a good mother, put another lump of sugar in his mouth, and then she offered him the glass again.

'I can't drink it like that,' said the puppet, making hundreds of grimaces.

'Why can't you?'

'Because that pillow on my feet annoys me.'

The fairy removed the pillow.

'It's no use. I can't drink it like that, either.'

'What is the matter now?'

'The door bothers me; it's half open.'

The fairy went and shut the door.

'The fact is,' cried Pinocchio, bursting into tears, 'I won't drink that bitter water – no, no, no . . .'

'My child, you will be sorry.'

'I don't care.'

'You are very ill.'

'I don't care.'

'This fever will send you to the other world in a few hours.'

'I don't care.'

'Are you not afraid to die?'

'Not a bit! I'd rather die than drink that horrid medicine!'

At that moment the door of the room opened, and four rabbits as black as ink came in, carrying a little black coffin on their shoulders.

'What do you want of me?' shouted Pinocchio, sitting up in his bed in terror.

'We have come to take you away,' said the biggest rabbit.

'To take me away! But I'm not dead yet!'

'No, not quite yet, but you have only a few minutes to live, because you refused the medicine that would have made you well.'

'O fairy, kind fairy,' cried the puppet, 'give me the glass at once; hurry, for Heaven's sake, for I don't want to die! No, I will not die!'

He took the glass in both hands, and emptied it at a draught.

'Ah, well!' said the rabbits. 'This time we have made a journey for nothing.' And taking the little coffin on their shoulders they left the room, murmuring and grumbling between their teeth.

A few minutes later Pinocchio jumped out of bed quite well; for you must know that wooden marionettes have the privilege of being ill very seldom and of getting well very quickly.

When the fairy saw him running and rushing about the room as gay and lively as a young rooster, she said, 'So my medicine really did do you good?'

'I should say so! It brought me back to life.'

'Then, for Heaven's sake, why was it so hard to make you drink it?'

'I think because we boys are all like that. We fear the medicine more than the sickness.'

'Shame on you! Boys should know that the right medicine, taken in time, might save them from a serious illness, perhaps even from death.'

'Oh, another time I won't make so much fuss. I'll remember those black rabbits with the coffin on their shoulders, and take the glass at once, and down it will go!'

'Now, come here, and tell me how it happened that you fell into the hands of assassins.'

'It was like this: the Showman, Fire-eater, gave me some gold pieces and said, "Here, take these to your father." But on the road I met the fox and the cat, two very decent people, and they said, "Would you like to change these pieces into a thousand – yes, into two thousand – gold pieces? Come with us, and we will take you to the Field of Miracles." So I said, "Let us go!" And they said, "Let's stop at the Red Crab Inn, and continue our way after midnight." And when I woke up they were not there, because they had left already. Then I started after them in the dark, and I couldn't tell you how dark it was. And so I met two assassins in coal sacks, who said to me, "Hand over your money!" And I said, "I haven't any", because I had hidden the four gold pieces in my mouth. One of the assassins tried to put his hand in my mouth, and I bit it off; but what I spat out wasn't a hand, but a cat's paw. And the assassins ran after me, and I ran and ran until they caught me, and hung me by the neck to a tree in the wood, saying, "We'll come back tomorrow, and then you will be dead, and your mouth will be open, and we'll get the money hidden under your tongue."'

'Where are the four gold pieces now?' asked the fairy.

'I've lost them,' answered Pinocchio. But he told a lie, for he had them in his pocket. No sooner had he told this lie than his nose, which was already very long, became two inches longer.

'Where did you lose them?'

'In the wood near by.'

At this second lie, his nose became still longer.

'If you lost them near here,' said the fairy, 'we can search for them; for everything lost in that wood can easily be found.'

'Oh! Now I remember everything,' replied the puppet, greatly confused. 'I didn't lose the money. I swallowed it when I was drinking your medicine.'

At this third lie, his nose grew so long that poor Pinocchio could not move in any direction. If he turned one way, his nose hit the bed or the window panes; if he turned the other, it struck the walls or the door; if he raised his head a little, there was danger of putting his nose into the fairy's eyes.

The fairy looked at him, and laughed.

'What are you laughing at?' asked the puppet, much embarrassed and worried about his nose, which was growing to such a size.

'I am laughing at the lies you have told.'

'How did you know I was telling lies?'

'Lies, my dear boy, can easily be recognized. There are two kinds of them: those with short legs, and those with long noses. Your kind have long noses.'

Pinocchio wanted to hide his face for shame. He tried to run out of the room, but he could not, for his nose was so long that he could not go through the door.

CHAPTER 18

Pinocchio again sees the fox and the cat and goes with them to sow his money in the Field of Miracles

As you may imagine, the fairy let the puppet scream and cry a good half hour because of his long nose which he could not get through the door. She did this to teach him a good lesson, and to correct him of the very bad habit of lying, which is one of the worst habits a boy can have. But when she saw his face disfigured from crying, and his eyes sticking out of his head, she pitied him. So she clapped her hands, at which signal a thousand big woodpeckers flew in at the window and, perching on Pinocchio's nose, pecked away at it with so much zeal that in a few minutes the big, ridiculous thing was reduced to its usual size.

'How good you are, dear fairy,' said the puppet, wiping his eyes. 'I love you so much!'

'I love you too,' answered the fairy, 'and if you want to stay with me, you shall be my little brother, and I will be your darling sister.'

'I'd like to stay with you, but what about my daddy?'

'I have thought of everything, and your father already knows everything. He will be here tonight.'

'Really?' exclaimed Pinocchio, jumping for joy. 'Then,

dearest fairy, if you don't mind, I shall go out to meet him. I can't wait any longer to see and kiss that poor old man, who has suffered so much for me!'

'Go, by all means, but don't get lost. Take the road through the wood, and you will surely meet him.'

Pinocchio left; and as soon as he reached the wood he began to run like a deer. At a certain place, in front of the big oak tree, he stopped, because he thought he heard people moving in the bushes. And indeed, there appeared all at once on the road – can you guess who? – the fox and the cat, his two travelling companions, with whom he had supped at the Red Crab Inn.

'Here is our dear Pinocchio,' exclaimed the fox, embracing and kissing him. 'How do you come to be here?'

'How do you come to be here?' repeated the cat.

'It's a very long story,' said the puppet. 'I'll tell it when I have time, though you should know this much – that the other night, when you left me alone in the inn, I encountered assassins on the road.'

'Assassins? Oh, my poor friend Pinocchio! And what did they want?'

'They wanted to rob me of my gold.'

'Infamous people!' said the fox.

'Most infamous people!' added the cat.

'But I ran away,' continued the puppet, 'and they chased me until they caught me, and hung me to a branch of that oak tree.' And Pinocchio pointed to the big oak.

'Did you ever hear anything more horrible!' said the fox. 'What a world we are condemned to live in! Where can honest people like us find shelter?'

While talking, Pinocchio noticed that the cat was lame of her right foreleg, since the paw with all its claws was missing. So he said to her, 'What has become of your paw?'

The cat wanted to say something, but got confused – so the fox answered quickly, 'My friend is too modest. That is why she doesn't answer, but I shall answer for her. About an hour ago we met an old wolf on the road, who was almost fainting from hunger. He asked alms of us, but we hadn't even a fish bone to give him; so what do you think my friend did – my friend, who has the heart of a Caesar? She bit off her own paw, and gave it to the poor beast, so that he could eat something.' As he told this, the fox wiped a tear.

Pinocchio was so deeply touched that he went to the cat, and whispered in her ear, 'If all cats were like you, mice would be fortunate creatures!'

'And what are you doing here?' asked the fox.

'I'm waiting for my father; he might come any moment.'

'And your gold pieces?'

'They are all in my pocket, except the one I spent at the inn of the Red Crab.'

'And to think that, by tomorrow, instead of four gold pieces they might be a thousand, or two thousand! Why not follow my advice, and bury them in the Field of Miracles?'

'Impossible, today. I'll go another time.'

'Another time will be too late,' said the fox.

'Why?'

'Because a rich man has bought the field, and after tomorrow nobody will be allowed to bury his money there.'

'How far away is the Field of Miracles?'

'Hardly two miles. Will you come with us? You will be there in half an hour, and bury your four gold pieces at once, and after a few minutes you shall have two thousand, and return in the evening with your pockets full. Will you come?'

Pinocchio remembered the good fairy, old Geppetto, and the warnings of the talking cricket; yet in the end he did as all boys do who have no sense, and no heart – that is, he shook his head and said to the fox and the cat, 'Let's go! I'll come with you.'

And off they went.

They had walked about half a day when they came to

a place called Fools' Trap. As soon as they entered the city, Pinocchio saw that the streets were full of dogs who had lost their hair, and whose mouths were wide open from hunger. There were shorn sheep, trembling with cold; roosters without their crests and combs, who were begging for a grain of maize; butterflies who could not fly, because they had sold their beautiful wings; peacocks without tails, who were ashamed to be seen; and pheasants who were crawling along, mourning for their beautiful gold and silver feathers, lost for ever.

In the midst of these beggars and shame-faced beasts, from time to time elegant carriages passed by, with a fox, or a thievish magpie, or some bird of prey inside.

'But where is the Field of Miracles?' asked Pinocchio.

'Just a few yards from here.'

They crossed the city and, going beyond the walls, they came to a lonely field that looked just like any other field.

'Here we are,' said the fox. 'Now, get to work and dig a small hole with your hands and put your gold pieces in.'

Pinocchio obeyed. He dug a hole, put into it the four gold pieces he still had, and covered them up with some earth.

'Now, then,' said the fox, 'go to the dam close by, bring a bucket of water, and water the ground where you have sown your fortune.'

Pinocchio went to the dam and, as he did not have a bucket, he took one of his old shoes, filled it with water, and watered the earth which covered his money.

'What else must I do?'

'Nothing else,' answered the fox. 'Now we can go away. You must come back in about twenty minutes, and you will see a little tree already growing through the earth, with its branches covered with money.'

The poor puppet was beside himself with joy, and he thanked the fox and the cat a thousand times, and promised them a lovely present.

'We don't want presents,' answered those two scoundrels. 'It's quite enough for us to have shown you how to get rich without hard work. That makes us as happy as can be.'

With these words they said good-bye to Pinocchio and, wishing him a splendid harvest, they went about their business.

CHAPTER 19

Pinocchio loses his money, and he is sent to prison where he spends four months

The puppet went back to the town, and started to count the minutes one by one. When he thought that twenty minutes were over he ran back to the Field of Miracles.

He ran as fast as he could, his heart beating like a grandfather clock – tick tock, tick tock – while he talked to himself.

'Suppose, instead of a thousand gold pieces, I find two thousand on the branches of the tree? Or instead of two thousand, five thousand? Or instead of five thousand, one hundred thousand? Oh, what a fine gentleman I shall be then! I shall have a magnificent palace, and a thousand wooden ponies and a thousand stables to play with, and a cellar full of lollies, and cordials, and a library brimful of candies, and tarts, and cakes, and almond biscuits, and cream puffs!'

While he was thus talking to himself, he came near the field, and stopped to look if he could see a tree, with branches laden with money; but he saw nothing. He went a little nearer – still nothing. He entered the field, went to the spot where he had buried his gold pieces, and still nothing at all. He stood there pondering; and, forgetting the rules and regulations of good manners, he took his hand out of his pocket, and scratched his head with all his might.

At that moment a loud laugh shattered the air and, looking up, he saw a large parrot sitting on a tree, cleaning the few feathers he had left.

'Why are you laughing?' asked Pinocchio angrily.

'I am laughing because while cleaning my feathers, I tickled myself under my wings.'

The puppet did not answer. He went to the dam, filled his old shoe with water again, and watered the earth covering his money.

While he did so, another laugh, more impertinent than the first one, rang out over the deserted field.

'I say!' shouted Pinocchio, angrily. 'May I know what you are laughing at, you ill-mannered parrot?'

'I am laughing at those simpletons who are silly enough to believe all the nonsense they hear, and who are always cheated by those who are more cunning than they are.'

'Are you, perhaps, speaking of me?'

'Yes, poor Pinocchio, I am, for you are so simple as to believe that you can sow and harvest money, like beans and pumpkins. There was a time when I believed that, too, and today I am suffering for it. Today – alas, it is too late – I have learnt that to earn money honestly, you must know how to do it with the labour of your hands, or with your brains.'

'I don't understand,' said the puppet, trembling with fear.

'Patience! I shall explain it plainer,' answered the parrot. 'While you were in the city, the fox and cat returned here; they dug out your money, and ran away like the wind. You must be a quick runner if you want to catch them.'

Pinocchio stood there with his mouth open, and as he did not believe what the parrot said, he began to dig up the earth he had watered. He dug, and dug, and dug, until he had a hole big enough for a haystack; but money there was none.

Then, in desperation, he ran back to the town, and went to the court house, to denounce the rascals who had robbed him.

The judge was an old gorilla, who was very old, and looked most respectable, with his white beard, but mostly for his gold spectacles without lenses, which he had to wear always because of an inflammation of the eyes, that he had had for many years.

In the judge's presence, Pinocchio told all the circumstances of the infamous fraud of which he had been the victim. He gave the names, surnames, and all other details of these rascals, and finished by demanding justice.

The judge, as he was very much interested in the story, listened to him with goodwill, and was extremely sorry for him. When the puppet had told everything, he stretched out his hand and rang a bell.

At the sound, two mastiffs appeared, dressed like policemen.

The judge pointed to Pinocchio and said, 'This poor fellow has been robbed of four gold pieces. Take him to the prison, immediately.'

Pinocchio was flabbergasted as he heard this sentence, which came like lightning out of a blue sky. He tried to protest, but the policemen did not want to waste any time, so they put their paws on his mouth, and took him to jail.

And there he remained for four months – four long months. And he would have remained longer had it not happened, fortunately, that the young Emperor of Fools' Trap, having won a big victory over his enemies, commanded a great public rejoicing. There were illuminations, fireworks, horse and bicycle races, and, first and foremost, he ordered the prisons to be opened, and every rascal to receive his freedom.

'If the others can go, I want to go too,' Pinocchio told the jailer.

'Oh no, you can't,' replied the jailer, 'for you are not in that class.'

'I beg your pardon,' said Pinocchio. 'I am a rascal, too.'

'In that case, you are perfectly right,' said the jailer, and taking off his cap respectfully, he bowed, opened the prison door, and let him out.

CHAPTER 20

When Pinocchio is freed from the prison he sets out for the fairy's house; but on the way he meets a horrible serpent, and afterwards is caught in a trap

Imagine Pinocchio's joy when he was free again! Without losing a second he left the town, and took the road that led to the fairy's little house.

Because it had been raining incessantly, the mud was knee-deep; but Pinocchio was not discouraged. He was so eager to meet his father again, and his little blue-haired sister, that he ran and jumped like a greyhound, and the mud splashed all over him.

As he ran he said to himself, 'How many dreadful things have happened to me! And I deserved them, for I am obstinate as a mule. I always wanted my own way, and never listened to those who loved me, and who had a thousand times more sense than I had. But from now I shall lead a different life, and become an obedient boy. I have learnt the lesson that disobedient children never prosper, and never gain anything. I wonder if my father is waiting for me? Shall I find him at the fairy's house? Poor Daddy! It's so long since I saw him, that I can hardly wait to embrace and kiss him. Will the fairy forgive me for disobeying her? Only to think of the good care she took of me, and the kindness she showed me! If I'm alive today I owe it to her. Could anyone imagine a more ungrateful or heartless boy than I am?'

Scarcely had he finished his pondering when he stopped, suddenly frightened, and went four steps back.

What had he seen? He saw a huge serpent stretched across the road. Its skin was green, its eyes were fiery, and its pointed tail smoked like a chimney.

You cannot imagine Pinocchio's terror. He went a long way back, and sat down on a little heap of stones, waiting for the serpent to go about his business, and leave the road free.

He waited an hour; two hours; three hours; but the serpent was still there, and even from far away he could see his glowing eyes, and the column of smoke coming from his tail.

At last Pinocchio took all his courage in both hands and, approaching the serpent, he said, in a very gentle, sweet, insinuating voice, 'Excuse me, Mr Serpent, but would you be so kind as to move on one side of the road, just enough for me to pass?'

He might as well have spoken to a wall. No one answered. He began again, with that same gentle voice, 'Consider, Mr Serpent, that I am going home, and my father is expecting me. It's such a long time since I have seen him! Would you let me pass on my way?'

He waited for some sign in answer to his request, but none came. On the contrary the serpent, who had until then appeared full of life, became perfectly quiet and almost rigid. He closed his eyes, and his tail stopped smoking. 'Maybe he is dead,' thought Pinocchio, rubbing his hands together joyfully, and, without further ado, he made to jump over him. But just as he was going to jump, the serpent rose suddenly like a spring; and the puppet, in his fright, jumped back, stumbled and fell.

It was a very clumsy fall, for his head got stuck in the mud, and his legs up in the air.

At the sight of that puppet standing on his head in the mud, and kicking with all his might, the serpent was seized with a fit of laughter; and he laughed, and laughed, and laughed, until he burst a blood vessel in his heart, and died.

And now Pinocchio started to run again as fast as he could, so as to reach the fairy's house before dark. But he got so terribly hungry that he jumped over a hedge into a field, to pick a few bunches of muscatel grapes. Would that he had not done it!

He had barely reached the vines, when – *Crack!* – his legs were caught by two sharp irons. The pain was so terrible that he saw countless stars of every hue, dancing in the sky. The poor puppet was caught in a trap put there to catch some big polecats that had been terrorizing all the poultry yards of the neighbourhood.

CHAPTER 21

Pinocchio is captured by a peasant who makes him work as a watchdog for his poultry yard

As you can imagine, Pinocchio began to scream and cry; but in vain, since there were no houses, and there was not a living soul to be seen on the road.

Meanwhile night came on.

Partly because of the pain caused by the trap which cut his leg, and partly because he was afraid to be alone in the dark, in the middle of the fields, Pinocchio almost fainted.

He saw a firefly above his head, and called to him, 'O little firefly, won't you be so kind as to free me from this torment?'

'Poor boy!' answered the firefly, looking at him with pity. 'How ever did you get caught in those sharp irons?'

'I came into the field to pick a few bunches of grapes, and . . .'

'But are they your grapes?'

'No . . .'

'And who ever taught you to take things that are not yours?'

'I was hungry . . .'

'Hunger, my child, is not a good excuse for taking what is not yours.'

'That's true, that's true,' said Pinocchio, 'I won't do it again.'

This conversation was interrupted by the sound of footsteps coming near. It was the owner of the field, coming on tiptoe to see if he had caught one of those polecats that were eating his chickens at night. When he took out his lantern from under his coat he was astonished to see that, instead of a polecat, he had caught a boy.

'Ah, you little thief!' the peasant said, angrily. 'So it's you who are eating my chickens!'

'It isn't I, it isn't I,' sobbed Pinocchio. 'I only came into the field to pick a few bunches of grapes!'

'He who will steal grapes will steal chickens too. Leave it to me! I'll teach you a lesson you'll remember for a while!'

He opened the trap, seized the puppet by the collar, and carried him off to his house as if he had been a lamb.

When he reached the yard in front of his house, he threw Pinocchio on the ground and, putting his foot on his neck, he said, 'It's late, and I want to go to bed. I shall settle your account tomorrow. Meanwhile, as my watchdog died today you shall take his place. You shall be my watchdog.'

Thereupon he put a heavy collar, covered with sharp brass knobs, on Pinocchio's neck, and fastened it so tightly that he could not slip his head through it. A long iron chain, attached to the collar, fixed it strongly to the wall.

'If it rains tonight,' said the peasant, 'you may go into that little kennel and lie down. You can use the straw that has served for four years as a bed for my poor dog. Remember to keep your ears pricked; and if, unluckily, thieves should come, don't forget to bark.'

With this last advice, the peasant went into the house and locked the door, leaving poor Pinocchio lying in the yard, more dead than alive with cold, hunger, and fright.

From time to time he put his fingers to the collar that pinched his throat, and said, crying, 'It serves me right! It serves me jolly well right! I wanted to be a good for nothing, and a vagabond. I listened to evil companions, so I have always been unlucky. If I had only been a good boy, like so many others – if I had been willing to study and to work, if I had stayed home with my poor father – I would not be here now in this lonely place, working as a watchdog for a peasant. Oh, if I could only be born again! But it's too late, now. I must have patience!'

This complaint, which came from the depth of his heart, relieved him a little. He crawled into the kennel, and fell asleep.

CHAPTER 22

Pinocchio discovers the thieves and, as a reward for his faithfulness, is set free

He had been sleeping soundly for over two hours, when, about midnight, he was wakened by the sound of strange voices that seemed to come from the yard. He stuck the point of his nose out of his kennel, and saw four animals with dark fur, that looked like cats. They were polecats – meat-eating animals, that are especially fond of eggs and young chickens. One of them, leaving his companions, came to the door of the kennel, and said in a low tone, 'Good evening, Melampo.'

'My name is not Melampo,' said the puppet.

'Who are you, then?'

'I am Pinocchio.'

'And what are you doing there?'

'I am a watchdog.'

'But where is Melampo? Where is the old dog that lived in this kennel?'

'He died this morning.'

'Did he? Poor beast! He was so kind! However, judging by your looks, you seem to be a good-natured dog, too!'

'Excuse me, I am not a dog!'

'Ah! What are you, then?'

'I am a puppet.'

'And you act as a watchdog?'

'Alas, I have to do it as a punishment!'

'Well, we might make the same bargain with you that we made with old Melampo. I'm sure our conditions will satisfy you.'

'And what might they be?'

'We shall come to the poultry yard one night a week, as in the past, and carry off eight chickens. We shall eat seven, and give you one, on condition, you must understand, that you pretend to be asleep when we are here, and never bark, or wake up the farmer.'

'Is that what Melampo did?'

'Yes, indeed, and we always got on splendidly together. Now sleep quietly, and you can be sure we shall bring you a chicken for your breakfast, ready plucked. Do we understand each other?'

'I understand only too clearly,' answered Pinocchio, shaking his head menacingly, as if saying, 'We'll soon see about that!'

When the four polecats thought they were safe, they went to the poultry yard, which was near the kennel. They opened the wooden door with their teeth and claws, and slipped inside, one after the other. But, scarcely were they all inside, when the door was shut with a loud bang.

It was Pinocchio who had shut it and, to make sure, he put a big stone against it.

Then he started to bark, and he barked just like a watchdog, 'Bow-wow-wow-wow!'

When the peasant heard him barking, he jumped out of bed and taking his gun, he came to the window, and called out, 'What's the matter?'

'The thieves are here!' cried Pinocchio.

'Where are they?'

'In the poultry yard.'

'I'm coming right away.'

Quicker than you can say 'Amen', the peasant had come. He went to the poultry yard, caught the four polecats and, putting them into a sack, he said with a pleased voice, 'At last you have fallen into my hands! I could punish you, but I am not so cruel. It is enough for me if I take you to the innkeeper in the village, who will skin you and cook you in a sweet-savoury sauce, and serve you for hares. It is an honour you do not deserve, but generous people like me are ready to do a good service.'

Then he went to Pinocchio, caressed him and, among other questions, he asked him, 'How did you discover these thieves? To think that Melampo, my faithful Melampo, never could find anything!'

The puppet could have told the truth – that is, he could have told the peasant of the shameful agreement between the dog and the polecats – but he remembered that the dog was dead, and he said to himself, 'What good will it do if I accuse the dead? A dead person is dead and gone. The best thing to do is to leave him in peace.'

'Were you awake, or asleep, when these rascals arrived?' asked the peasant.

'I was asleep,' answered Pinocchio, 'but they woke me by talking loudly, and one of them even came to my kennel, and said, "If you promise not to bark, or wake up the peasant, we shall give you a nicely plucked chicken." Imagine the impudence, offering such a proposition! I may be a puppet, and I may be full of faults, but I would never go with thieves, nor take a share in stolen goods!'

'Good for you, my boy!' said the peasant, patting him on the shoulder. 'Such sentiments do credit to you. And to show how grateful I am, I give you back your freedom, that you may go home.' And he took off the dog's collar.

CHAPTER 23

Pinocchio weeps for the death of the beautiful blue-haired child; then he meets a pigeon who carries him to the seashore, where he dives into the water to save his father

When Pinocchio was freed from that heavy, humiliating collar on his neck, he started out across the fields, never stopping for a second until he reached the road which led to the fairy's house.

When he reached it, he stopped to look down on the countryside. He could see plainly, with his naked eye, the site where he unluckily met the fox and the cat. He could see the wood with the big oak on which he had been hanged; but, although he looked everywhere, he could not see the little house where the lovely blue-haired child had lived.

Driven by a sad foreboding, he ran with all his might and in a few minutes he reached the field where the little white house had once stood. But the little white house was no longer there. Instead there was a little piece of white marble on which these sad words were engraved:

HERE LIES
THE BLUE-HAIRED CHILD
WHO DIED OF SORROW
ON BEING DESERTED BY HER

LITTLE BROTHER
PINOCCHIO

I leave you to imagine the puppet's feelings when he had spelt out this inscription. He fell to the ground and, kissing the cold stone a thousand times, burst into a flood of tears. He cried all night, and at dawn he was still crying, although he had no more tears. His wailing and moaning were so loud and penetrating that it was echoed from all the neighbouring hills.

As he wept he said, 'O dear fairy, why are you dead? Why didn't I die – I who am so wicked – instead of you, who were so good? And my father, where is he? O dear little fairy, tell me where I can find him, for I want to stay with him for ever, and never, never leave him. Dear fairy, tell me it is not true that you are dead! If you really love me, if you love your little brother, come to life just once more; come back as you were before! Are you not sorry to see me here alone, abandoned by everybody? Should the assassins come again, they will hang me, and then I shall be dead for ever. What can I do, alone in the world? Now that I have lost you, and my father, who will look after me? Where shall I sleep? Who will make me a new jacket? Oh, it will be better, a hundred times better, if I die too! Yes, I want to die! Boo-hoo-hoo!' In this desperate state he tried to tear his hair, but as it was made of wood, he could not even stick his fingers through it.

At this moment a large pigeon, flying high above him, stopped with outstretched wings, and called to him, 'Tell me, child, what are you doing down there?'

'Don't you see? I'm crying!' said Pinocchio, looking towards the voice, and rubbing his eyes with his jacket.

'Tell me,' continued the pigeon, 'do you know, among your friends, a puppet called Pinocchio?'

'Pinocchio? Did you say Pinocchio?' shouted the puppet, jumping to his feet. 'I'm Pinocchio!'

At this answer, the pigeon quickly alighted to the ground. He was larger than a turkey. 'Do you know Geppetto, too?' he asked.

'Do I know him? He is my poor father! Has he spoken to you of me? Will you take me to him? Is he still alive? Tell me quickly, for Heaven's sake, is he still alive?'

'I left him three days ago on the sea coast.'

'What was he doing?'

'He was making a little boat to cross the ocean in. The poor man has been wandering around the world more than three months, and looking for you. As he couldn't find you, he decided to search for you in distant countries.'

'How far is it from here to the sea coast?' Pinocchio asked anxiously.

'Nearly six hundred miles.'

'Nearly six hundred miles? O dear pigeon, what a fine thing it would be if I had wings like you.'

'If you want to go, I shall carry you.'

'How?'

'Astride on my back. Are you very heavy?'

'Heavy? No, indeed! I'm as light as a feather.'

Without wasting another word, Pinocchio jumped on the pigeon's back, with a leg on each side of him like a rider on a horse, and shouted gaily, 'Gallop, gallop, little horse, for I'm in a terrible hurry!'

The pigeon took flight, and in a few minutes he was so high that they almost touched the clouds. Once at that great height, the puppet grew very curious, and looked down; but he got so frightened, and the sight made him so dizzy, that he put his arms tight around the neck of his feathered steed to save himself from falling off. They flew all day.

Towards evening, the pigeon said, 'I am so thirsty!'

'And I am so hungry!' added Pinocchio.

'Let us stop a few minutes at this dovecote; then we shall continue our flight, and by dawn we shall be at the sea coast.'

They entered a deserted dovecote, where there was nothing but a basin of water, and a basket full of green seed.

The puppet had never in his life been able to eat green seed, for, as he said, it turned his stomach; but that evening he could not eat enough of it, and when the basket was empty he said to the pigeon, 'I couldn't have believed green seed could taste so good!'

'You will learn, my lad,' replied the pigeon, 'that when you are really hungry, and there is nothing else to eat, even green seed becomes delicious. Hunger is the best cook.'

After having finished this little meal they did not rest, but continued their journey. The next morning they arrived at the seashore.

The pigeon stopped to let Pinocchio dismount, and then quickly flew away. He did not want to be thanked for having done a good deed.

The beach was full of people, who were shouting and gesticulating as they looked out to the sea.

'What's happened?' Pinocchio asked of an old woman.

'A poor father has lost his son, and he intends crossing the sea in a small boat, to search for him; but the waves are so high that the boat will capsize.'

'Where is the boat?'

'Right there, where my finger points,' said the old woman, pointing to a little boat which, at that distance, looked like a nutshell with a very small man in it.

Pinocchio looked closely, and uttered a piercing cry, 'It's my father! It's my father!'

Meanwhile the little boat, thrown by the angry waves, once disappeared completely, then reappeared on the top of a wave. Pinocchio, standing on a high rock, called his father by name, again and again, signalling with his hands, with his cap, and with his handkerchief.

Although Geppetto was very far away, he seemed to recognize his son, for he waved with his cap, and he also made signs as if he would like to return to land; but the sea was so furious that he could not use his oars.

Suddenly there came a huge wave, and the little boat disappeared. They waited to see it again.

'Poor man!' said the fishermen, who were standing together on the beach. And murmuring a prayer they turned to go home.

Suddenly they heard a desperate shout and looking back, they saw a boy jumping into the sea from a rock, crying, 'I will save my father!'

Pinocchio, being made of wood, floated easily, and swam like a fish. They saw him disappear under the water, beaten about by the waves, and then he reappeared. In the distance, now a leg appeared, now an arm, but at last they lost sight of him altogether.

'Poor boy!' said the fishermen on the beach; and, murmuring a prayer, they went home.

CHAPTER 24

Pinocchio arrives at Busy Bee Island and finds the fairy again

Hoping to arrive in time to save his poor father, Pinocchio swam all night.

And what a terrible night it was! The rain came down like a flood, with hailstones and terrible thunderclaps, while flashes of lightning made the world as bright as day.

Towards morning, he saw in the distance a long strip of land. It was an island in the midst of the sea.

He tried in vain to reach the shore, the tumbling waves tossed him everywhere, as if he were straw or a stick. At last, happily, there came a huge wave that carried him out and threw him violently on the shore. He struck the shore with such force that all his ribs and joints rattled; but he comforted himself by saying, 'That was another miraculous escape!'

Slowly, slowly the clouds cleared, the sun came out in all his splendour, and the sea became as quiet and smooth as oil.

The puppet spread his clothes to dry in the sun, and began looking in every direction over that huge expanse of water to see if there was a small boat anywhere with a small man in it. But although he looked and looked, he saw only the sky and the sea, and the sails of some ships; but they were so far away that they looked no bigger than flies.

'I wish I knew the name of this island!' he said. 'If only I could know that decent people lived here, who do not hang boys on trees! But is there nobody I can ask all these questions?'

The idea of being alone, all alone in a country where nobody lived, made him so melancholy that he was just about to cry when he saw a big fish near the shore, swimming by. It was quietly going about its own business with its head out of water.

Since he did not know its name, he cried loudly, 'Hullo, Mr Fish. May I have a word with you?'

'Even two, if you like,' answered the fish, who was a dolphin, but so polite that there were few like him in the seas of the world.

'Would you be so kind as to tell me if there are inhabited places on this island, where one may eat without fear of being eaten?'

'Certainly there are,' answered the dolphin. 'There is one not very far from here.'

'Which road will lead me there?'

'Take the path on your left, and follow your nose. You can't make a mistake.'

'Tell me something else. You swim in the sea all day and all night. Have you, by chance, seen a small boat with my father in it?'

'Who is your father?'

'He is the best father in the world; and I am very likely the worst son.'

'As we had a very bad storm last night,' said the dolphin, 'the boat was probably sunk.'

'And my father?'

'By this time he must have been eaten by the huge shark that has been spreading death and misery in these waters for a long time.'

'Is he very big, this shark?' asked Pinocchio, frightened and trembling.

'Is he big?' asked the dolphin. 'Well, just to give you an idea, I shall merely tell you that he is larger than a five-storey house, and his mouth is so wide and deep that it would easily hold a railway train, with its engine smoking and all.'

'Heavens above!' cried the terrified puppet and, dressing quickly, he turned to the dolphin saying, 'Good-bye, Mr Fish, excuse the trouble I have caused you, and many thanks for your kindness.'

Then he hurried down the little path, almost running. At the least noise he looked behind him, fearing to see that horrible shark as large as a five-storey house, and with a railway train in his mouth, pursuing him.

He had travelled about half an hour when he came to Busy Bee town. On the streets people were hurrying back and forth, on business. Everybody had something to do; everybody was working; you could not have found an idler or a tramp if you had searched with a lamp.

'I see,' lazy Pinocchio told himself, 'that this place will never do for me. I was not born for work.'

By this time he was terribly hungry, for he had had nothing to eat for more than twenty-four hours, not even a dish of green seeds.

What could he do? To get some food, there were only two ways: ask for work, or beg for pennies or bread.

He was ashamed to beg. His father had told him several times that only the aged and the crippled have a right to beg. Poor, really poor in this world – those who really deserve help and pity – are those who, by reason of old age or sickness, are no longer able to earn their living by their own labour. It is everybody else's duty to work; and if they refuse to work, and are hungry, so much the worse for them.

Just at that moment a man passed by, tired and panting.

He was pulling, with great difficulty, two carts loaded with charcoal.

Pinocchio judged, by his look, that he was a kind man; so he approached him and, casting his eyes downward in shame, he said in a low tone, 'Will you please give me a penny, for I am dying of hunger.'

'Not only one penny,' answered the man, 'but I shall give you two, if you'll help me draw home these loads of charcoal.'

'I am surprised at you!' answered Pinocchio, offended. 'Let me tell you that I am not a donkey! I do not draw carts.'

'That's all right!' the coal dealer answered. 'But then, my boy, if you are really so hungry, eat a couple of slices of your pride, and take care you don't get indigestion!'

A few minutes later a mason passed by, carrying a load of lime on his shoulder.

'Sir, would you be so kind as to give a penny to a poor boy who is hungry?'

'With pleasure. Come with me and carry lime,' answered the bricklayer, 'and instead of one penny, I shall give you five.'

'But lime is so heavy,' objected Pinocchio, 'and I don't want to get tired.'

'If you don't want to get tired, my boy, amuse yourself with being hungry, and much good may it do you!'

In less than half an hour twenty people passed by, and Pinocchio begged of all of them, but they all answered, 'Are you not ashamed? Instead of begging on the road, go to work, and earn your living!'

At last a kind little woman appeared carrying two pails of water.

'Kind lady, will you let me have a drink of water from your pail?' asked Pinocchio, who was burning with thirst.

'Yes, drink, my child,' said the little woman, putting the pails down.

When Pinocchio had had a good drink, he wiped his

mouth, and said, 'Now I'm thirsty no more. If only I were no longer hungry!'

The good woman, hearing these words, said quickly, 'If you carry one of these pails home, I'll give you a big piece of bread.'

Pinocchio looked at the pail, and said neither yes nor no.

'And with the bread, I shall give you a nice dish of cauliflower, with oil and vinegar,' added the good woman.

Pinocchio looked at the pail again, but he did not say yes or no.

'And after cauliflower, I shall give you some tasty sweets.'

This last temptation Pinocchio could not resist; and he said resolutely, 'All right, then! I will carry the pail home for you.'

The pail was very heavy, and, his hands not being strong enough to hold it, the puppet had to put it on his head.

When they arrived home, the good woman led Pinocchio to a little table already set, and put the bread, the cauliflower, and the sweets before him.

Pinocchio did not eat like a human being: he gobbled everything. His stomach was like a tenement house that had been uninhabited for five months.

Bite by bite his hunger was appeased, and he raised his head to thank his benefactress. Immediately he looked at her he uttered a long 'O-o-o-oh!' of astonishment, and sat there with his fork in the air, his mouth full of bread and cauliflower, his eyes wide open as if he had been bewitched.

'What is the matter with you?' asked the good woman, laughing.

'Because, it's . . .' stammered Pinocchio, 'it's . . . it's . . . you are like . . . you remind me of . . . Yes, yes, yes. The same voice . . . the same eyes . . . the same hair . . . You have blue hair, too, just as she had! O dear fairy, O dear fairy, tell me, is it you? Is it really you? Don't make me cry any more! If you only knew! I have cried so much, I have suffered so much!'

As he said this, Pinocchio fell on his knees before her, and threw his arms round that mysterious little woman, and began to cry bitterly.

CHAPTER 25

Pinocchio promises the fairy to be good and study, because he is tired of being a puppet and wishes to become a really good boy

At first the little woman would not admit that she was the blue-haired fairy, but seeing that she had been found out, and not wishing to continue the comedy any longer, she acknowledged the fact, saying to Pinocchio, 'You rascal of a puppet, how did you recognize me?'

'It was my love for you that told me.'

'Do you remember? When you left me I was a little girl, and now I am a woman, nearly old enough to be your mother.'

'I like that very much, because instead of calling you little sister, I shall call you mother. I've always wanted to have a mother, as other boys. But how did you manage to grow so quickly?'

'That's a secret.'

'Teach it me! I would like to be a little bigger. Look at me! I've never been more than a Tom Thumb.'

'But you can't grow,' answered the fairy.

'Why not?'

'Because puppets never grow. They are born puppets, they live puppets and they die puppets.'

'I'm sick of always being a puppet!' cried Pinocchio,

slapping his wooden head. 'It's about time I became a man, like other people!'

'If you only deserved it, you could become one.'

'Really? And what can I do to deserve to become a man?'

'It's very easy: you begin by being a good boy.'

'Why? Do you mean to say that I'm not a good boy?'

'You are anything but! Good boys are obedient, and you . . .'

'I am never obedient.'

'Good boys like to work and study, and you . . .'

'And I am an idle vagrant all the year round.'

'Good boys always tell the truth . . .'

'And I always tell lies.'

'Good boys like to go to school . . .'

'And school gives me a pain. But from this day forward, I shall turn over a new leaf.'

'Do you promise to do that?'

'Yes, I do. I shall be a good little boy, and be the consolation of my father. Where can my poor father be?'

'I don't know.'

'Will I ever be lucky enough to see him again?'

'I hope so. Yes, I am sure of it.'

Hearing this, Pinocchio was so happy that he took the fairy's hands and kissed them, almost mad with joy. Then, looking up at her with loving eyes, he said, 'Tell me, mother dear, it wasn't true, then, that you were dead?'

'It seems not,' answered the fairy, smiling.

'If you only knew how sad I was and how my heart ached, when I read: "here lies . . ."!'

'I know, and that is why I have forgiven you. As you were really sorry, I knew that you had a good heart; and if a child has a good heart, even if he is mischievous and full of bad habits, there is hope that he will mend his ways. That is why I came here to look for you. I shall be your mamma . . .'

'Oh, lovely!' shouted Pinocchio, jumping for joy.

'You must always obey me, and do as you are told.'

'Oh yes, yes, yes!'

'Tomorrow,' added the fairy, 'you will start to go to school.'

Pinocchio grew a little less joyful.

'Then you will choose some profession or trade, which-ever you would like . . .'

Pinocchio made a wry face.

'What are you muttering between your teeth?' asked the fairy, angrily.

'I was saying,' grumbled Pinocchio, 'that it seems to me too late for me to go to school now.'

'No, my lad! Remember always that it's never too late to learn and get educated.'

'But I don't want to learn any profession or trade . . .'

'Why not?'

'Because I don't like work.'

'My child,' said the fairy, 'people who talk like that gener-ally end in a hospital, or in a prison. Remember that every man, rich or poor, must find something to do in this world; everybody must work. Woe to those who lead idle lives! Idleness is a dreadful disease, of which one should be cured immediately in childhood; if not, one never gets over it.'

These words touched Pinocchio's heart. He lifted his head quickly, and said to the fairy, 'I will study, I will work. I will do everything you tell me, for I am sick of being a puppet. I want to become a real boy, whatever I have to do for it. You promised that I could, didn't you?'

'Yes, it's true, I promised, and now it depends on you.'

CHAPTER 26

Pinocchio and his schoolmates go to the seashore to see the terrible shark

Next day Pinocchio went to school. Imagine what those mischievous boys did when they saw a puppet coming to their school! It seemed as if their laughter would never come to an end. One took his cap away, another pulled his jacket behind. One of the boys tried to make a big moustache under his nose with ink, and another again tried to tie strings to his hands and feet, to make him dance.

Pinocchio pretended not to notice them at first; but at last he lost his patience and, turning to his worst teasers, he told them menacingly, 'Take care, boys! I didn't come here to be your clown! I respect others, and I want to be respected.'

'Good for you, peacock! You talk like a book!' howled the rogues, laughing more than ever; and one of them, more impertinent than the others, put out his hand to seize the puppet's nose.

But he was not quick enough, for Pinocchio kicked his shins under the table.

'Oh! Oh! What hard feet!' cried the boy, rubbing the bruises on his aching shins.

'And what elbows! They're even harder than his feet!'

exclaimed another, who had received a blow in the stomach for his rude jokes.

After a few kicks and blows, Pinocchio won the respect and liking of the whole school, and they all made friends with him.

Even the master praised him, because he was attentive, studious, and intelligent, first to arrive at school, and the last to leave when school was over.

His only fault was that he made too many friends. Some of these friends were well known as good-for-nothings, unwilling to study. The master warned him daily, and the good fairy never failed to repeat it.

'Be careful, Pinocchio! Those bad friends of yours will end up by making you lose your love for our books. I hope they won't lead you into any great trouble.'

'Oh, there's no such danger!' answered the puppet, shrugging his shoulders, and touching his forehead with his finger as if to say, 'There's too much good sense here inside!'

Now, it happened one day, as he was on his way to school, that he met some of these friends, who asked him, 'Have you heard the great news?'

'No.'

'They say that, not far away from here, there's a shark in the sea as big as a mountain.'

'You don't say so! I wonder if it's the same shark that was there on the night when my poor father was drowned?'

'We're going to the beach to see it. Will you come too?'

'Not I! I'm going to school.'

'Why should you go to school? We can go to school tomorrow. One lesson more or less won't change us, we'll still remain the same blockheads.'

'But what will the master say?'

'He can say what he likes. He is paid to find fault all day long.'

'And my mother?'

'Oh, mothers never find out anything,' answered those wicked boys.

'I know what I'll do,' said Pinocchio. 'I have certain reasons for seeing the shark, but I'll go after school.'

'You poor blockhead!' said one of them. 'Do you think a fish of that size will wait for you? When he's tired of being in one place, he'll go to another, and then that'll be that!'

'How long does it take to go to the beach?' asked the puppet.

'We can be there and back in an hour.'

'Well, come on then! Whoever runs fastest is the best chap!' cried Pinocchio.

At this starting sign, all the boys ran across the fields, with their books and slates under their arms. Pinocchio led them, for he ran as if he had wings on his feet.

From time to time he turned to poke fun at his friends, who were a long way behind him; and when he saw them panting, covered with dust, and with their tongues hanging, he laughed heartily. The poor boy did not guess at that moment, what terrors and dreadful disasters were awaiting him.

CHAPTER 27

Great battle between Pinocchio and his friends, during which one of them is wounded and Pinocchio is arrested

When he arrived at the shore, Pinocchio looked at the sea, but he saw no shark. The sea was as smooth as a great mirror.

'Well, where's the shark?' he asked, turning to his friends.

'Perhaps he has gone to breakfast,' said one of them, laughing.

'Or perhaps he went to bed to have a nap,' said another, laughing still louder.

Their silly answers and stupid laughter told Pinocchio that it was all a joke, and that he had believed a lie. He was very angry, and he said indignantly, 'May I know what your idea was in telling me that story about the shark?'

'It was great fun, to be sure!' the rogues answered in chorus.

'Well, what was it?'

'We wanted you to stay away from school, and come with us. Aren't you ashamed to be so proper and industrious every day? Aren't you ashamed to study so hard?'

'And why should you mind how hard I study?'

'We mind it because you make us look so small in the master's eyes.'

'Why?'

'Because boys who study always make those who don't small by comparison, and we don't like it. We have some pride, too.'

'What can I do, then, to please you?'

'You must do as we do, and hate the school, and the lessons, and the master – our three great enemies.'

'And suppose I choose to keep on studying?'

'Then we'll have nothing to do with you, and we'll take the very first chance to get even with you!'

'Really, you make me laugh,' said the puppet, shaking his head.

'Take care, Pinocchio,' said one of the big boys, facing him. 'Don't think you can lord it over us! Don't think you can crow over us! If you aren't afraid of us, we're not afraid of you. Remember you're alone, and we are seven.'

'Seven, like the seven deadly sins,' said Pinocchio laughing.

'Did you hear that? He has insulted us. He has called us the seven deadly sins!'

'Pinocchio, say you're sorry, or it will be the worse for you!'

'Coo-coo!' said the puppet, putting his outstretched fingers to his nose.

'Pinocchio, you'll be sorry!'

'Coo-coo!'

'We'll beat you like a donkey!'

'Coo-coo!'

'You'll go home with a broken nose!'

'Coo-coo!'

'I'll give you "Coo-coo"!' shouted the most daring of the boys. 'Take this for a start, and keep it for supper!' With this, he gave him a blow on the head.

But it was, as the saying goes, give and take, for the puppet, as was to be expected, returned the blow, and in a moment the fight became general and furious.

Pinocchio was alone, but he defended himself like a hero. His hard wooden feet kept his enemies at a respectful distance. Wherever those feet touched, they left a black mark that would not easily be forgotten.

The bad boys, angry because they could not get near Pinocchio, began to use other weapons. They unstrapped their school bags, and began to throw their books, primers and grammars, dictionaries, geography and other school books. But the puppet had sharp eyes, and dodged so quickly, that the books all flew over his head into the sea.

What do you suppose the fish did? Thinking those books were something to eat, they came in shoals; but hardly had they tasted a page or two, or a cover page, when they spat it out again, with a grimace that seemed to say, 'We are used to much better food than this!'

The fight was growing more furious when suddenly a big crab that had come out of the water and climbed on to the beach called loudly, in a voice like a trumpet with a cold, 'Stop it, you rascals! These schoolboy fights always end badly. Something bad will surely happen!'

Poor crab! He might as well have preached to the wind. Pinocchio was no better than the rest, and said rudely to him, 'Shut up, you detestable crab! Take rather some lozenges for the cold in your throat! Go to bed, and take some medicine!'

Just then the boys, who had thrown away all their own books, saw Pinocchio's school bag lying on the ground, and in less time than it takes to tell it they took possession of it.

Among the books there was a large one bound in strong board, with leather back and corners. It was a *Treatise on Arithmetic*. You can imagine for yourselves how heavy and large it must have been!

One of these rascals seized the volume, and threw it at Pinocchio's head, with all the force he could muster. But, instead of hitting the puppet, it struck one of his own friends on the head.

The child turned as white as a sheet, and shouted, 'Oh, Mamma, help me! I am dying!' And fell his full length on the sand.

At that, the frightened boys ran away, and in a few moments they were out of sight.

But Pinocchio stayed there, and although from sorrow and fright he was more dead than alive, he wet his handkerchief in the sea, and put it on the poor boy's temples, weeping bitterly, calling him by name, and saying, 'Eugene! Poor Eugene! Open your eyes and look at me! Why don't you answer? I didn't hurt you! Believe me, it wasn't I! Open your eyes, Eugene. If you keep them shut, I shall die too. Alas! Alas! What shall I do? How shall I have the courage to go back to my mother? What will become of me? Where can I fly to hide myself? Oh, how many thousand times better would it have been if I had gone to school! Why did I listen to bad friends? They are my ruin! The master told me so, and my mother said, "Beware of evil companions!" But I am obstinate . . . and a fool. I listen to them . . . and then do as I please! And afterwards, I have to suffer for it. It has always been so since I was born. I've never had a really good quarter of an hour in my life. Oh dear, oh dear, what will become of me?'

Pinocchio was still crying, moaning, and striking his head, and calling Eugene, when suddenly he heard approaching footsteps. He turned, and saw two policemen.

'What are you doing there on the ground?' they asked the puppet.

'I am helping my schoolmate.'

'Is anything wrong with him?'

'I think so.'

'No doubt about it!' said one of the policemen, bending over Eugene, and looking at him closely. 'This boy is wounded on the temple. Who did it?'

'Not I,' stammered Pinocchio, frightened.

'If it wasn't you, who was it then?'

'Not I,' repeated Pinocchio.

'What was he wounded with?'

'With this book.'

The puppet picked up the *Treatise on Arithmetic*, bound in board and leather, and showed it to the policeman.

'And whose book is this?'

'Mine.'

'That's enough; there's no more to say. Get up, and come with us!'

'But I . . .'

'Come along!'

'But I am innocent . . .'

'Come along!'

Before leaving, the policemen called some fishermen who were rowing near the shore, and said to them, 'We are leaving this wounded boy with you. Take him home and look after him. We shall be back tomorrow.'

Then they turned to Pinocchio, who had to walk between them, and they said as a military command, 'Forward! And step lively, or it will be much the worse for you!'

Without waiting for them to repeat it, the puppet set out on the path that led to the village. The poor puppet did not know where his head was, but thought he was dreaming a dreadful dream. He was almost beside himself. His eyes saw double, his legs trembled, his tongue stuck to the roof of his mouth, so that he could not speak. Yet in the midst of his awe and bewilderment there was one thought that pierced his tormented heart like a thorn; the thought that he would have to pass under the good fairy's windows between two policemen. He would rather have died.

They had just entered the village when the wind blew off Pinocchio's cap, and carried it some ten yards away.

'Do you mind if I go and get my cap?' Pinocchio asked the policeman.

'Yes, go, but hurry.'

The puppet picked up his cap, but instead of putting it on his head, he took it between his teeth, and began running towards the sea.

Thinking it would be hard to catch him, the policeman sent a big mastiff after him, that had won the first prizes in all the dog races. Pinocchio ran, but the dog ran faster. People all came to the windows, or ran down the street, to see the end of that fierce race. But they could not see it, for Pinocchio and the dog raised so much dust on the street that in a few minutes nothing could be seen.

CHAPTER 28

Pinocchio is in danger of being fried as a fish

There was a moment during this fierce race when Pinocchio felt himself lost; for you must know that Alidoro – that was the mastiff's name – had almost caught him.

The puppet could hear the dreadful beast panting close behind him; they were separated only by inches, and he even felt its hot breath.

Fortunately, by this time, he was near the beach, and it was only a few steps to the sea.

As soon as he reached the shore the puppet jumped, like a frog, and he was far out in the water. Alidoro wanted to stop, but as he was going so fast he was carried out into the water, too. Unfortunately he could not swim, so he pawed desperately, trying to keep his nose above water; but the more he tried, the more he went under.

When he rose to the surface his eyes were almost jumping out of his head, and he barked, 'I'm drowning! I'm drowning!'

'Drown, then!' answered Pinocchio, who was now a good distance away, and out of all danger.

'Help me, Pinocchio! Save my life! Oh! Oh!'

At that desperate cry the puppet, who was really very kind-hearted, took pity on him and, turning to the dog, he said, 'If I save your life, do you promise not to bother me any more, or run after me?'

'I promise! I promise! Be quick, for pity's sake, for in another half-minute I'll be dead!'

Pinocchio still hesitated, but then he remembered his father's saying that no one ever loses by doing a good deed. He swam to Alidoro and holding him by the tail with both hands, he pulled him safe and sound to the dry sandy beach.

The poor dog could not stand up. He had drunk, in spite of himself, so much salt water that he was like a balloon. However, the puppet did not dare to trust him completely, so he thought it better to jump into the sea again.

As he swam away he called to the friend he had rescued, 'Good-bye, Alidoro! A good journey to you, and give my love at home.'

'Good-bye, Pinocchio!' answered the dog. 'A thousand thanks for saving my life. You were very kind to me, and in this world one good deed deserves another. Should you ever need me, I shall remember you.'

Pinocchio went on swimming, keeping near the shore. At last, he thought he had reached a safe place. Looking round the beach, he saw a cave among the rocks, with a long column of smoke coming out of it.

'There must be a fire in that cave,' he said to himself. 'So much the better! I can warm and dry myself, and then? And then we shall see.'

Having come to this decision, he swam near the rocks. But just as he was climbing out, he felt something rising under the water, and it lifted him out on the beach. He tried to escape, but it was too late, for, to his great surprise, he found himself in a big net, among a huge number of fish of every shape and size, flapping and jumping as if they were all mad.

At the same time he saw, coming out of the cave, a fisherman who was so ugly that he looked like a sea monster. Instead of hair, there grew on his head a bush thickly covered with green leaves. His skin was green, his eyes were green, and his long beard that reached to the ground was green. He looked like a huge green lizard, standing on his hind legs.

When the fisherman had taken the net out of the sea, he shouted joyfully, 'Thank Heaven! I shall have a fine meal of fish today!'

'How lucky I am not to be a fish,' said Pinocchio to himself, having gathered a little courage.

The net full of fish was taken into the cave, which was dark and smoky and in the middle of it there was a big frying-pan full of boiling oil, which smelled so strongly that it nearly took one's breath away.

'Now we shall see the fish we've caught!' said the green fisherman, and, putting one of his big, misshapen hands, which looked like bakers' shovels, into the net, he took out a handful of mullet.

'These mullet will be good!' he said, looking at them, and smelling them with anticipation. Then he threw them into a pan without any water.

He repeated this operation several times; and, as he drew out the fish, his mouth watered, and he said joyfully, 'These whiting will be excellent! . . . These sardines are exquisite! . . . These crabs will be excellent! . . . These anchovies will be fine!'

As you may imagine, the whiting, the sardines, the crabs, and the anchovies all went together into the dish, to keep the mullet company.

The last in the net was Pinocchio.

When the fisherman pulled him out, he opened wide his green eyes, and cried, almost frightened, 'What kind of fish is this? I have never tasted such a fish!'

Having looked him over carefully several times, he finished by saying, 'I see: it must be a crab.'

Pinocchio was hurt at being mistaken for a crab, and he said indignantly. 'What do you mean by calling me a crab? Nice way to treat me! Let me tell you, I'm a puppet.'

'A puppet?' said the fisherman. 'In truth, a puppet fish is new to me. All the better! I shall eat you with very great pleasure!'

'Eat me? Will you understand once and for all that I am not a fish? Don't you see that I can talk and reason as you do?'

'That's right,' answered the fisherman. 'And now, seeing you are a fish that can speak and reason as I do, I shall treat you with the greatest consideration.'

'And what will that be?'

'As a token of friendship, and particular consideration, I shall let you choose the way how you should be cooked. Would you prefer to be fried in oil in a pan, or stewed with tomato sauce?'

'To tell the truth,' answered Pinocchio, 'if I must choose, I'd prefer to get back my freedom, and go home.'

'You're joking! How can you think I'd lose this chance to taste such a rare fish? You don't catch puppet fish every day. Leave it to me: I shall fry you in the pan with all the other fish, and you'll be quite happy. To be fried in company is always a consolation.'

Hearing this, the miserable Pinocchio cried and screamed, and begged for mercy, sobbing, 'How much better it would have been if I had gone to school! I pay dearly for listening to such friends! OH! Oh! Oh!' And because he wriggled like an eel, and made every effort to escape from the green fisherman's hands, the fisherman took a long bulrush and, binding him hand and foot like a sausage, threw him into the dish with the others.

Then he got a wooden jar full of flour, and began rolling all the fish in it; and as fast as he was done with them, he threw them into the frying-pan.

The first to dance in the boiling oil were the poor whiting; then came the crabs, the sardines, the sole, and the anchovies. At last it was Pinocchio's turn, who, being so near death – and such a terrible death – trembled so much, and was so frightened, that he could no longer find voice or even breath to beg for mercy.

The poor boy could only beg with his eyes; but the green fisherman, without even looking at him, rolled him over five or six times in the flour, covering him so completely that he looked like a puppet made of plaster. Then he took him by the head and . . .

CHAPTER 29

*Pinocchio goes back to the fairy's house;
she promises him that the next day he will
no longer be a puppet, but a boy; grand
breakfast of coffee and milk to celebrate
the coming event*

Just as the fisherman was about to throw Pinocchio into the
frying-pan, a big dog entered the cave, drawn there by
the strong, delicious odour of fried fish.

'Get out!' ordered the fisherman, threatening him, and
still holding the floury puppet in his hand.

But the poor dog was starving, and he howled, and
wagged his tail as if to say, 'Just give me one mouthful of fish,
and I'll go away.'

'Get out, I tell you!' repeated the fisherman, getting
ready to kick him.

But the dog was far too hungry to care about being
kicked, and growling at the fisherman, he showed his sharp
teeth.

Just then, a faint little voice was heard in the cave saying,
'Save me, Alidoro! If you don't save me, I shall be fried!'

The dog at once recognized Pinocchio's voice, and he
was amazed to see that it came from that floury bundle in
the fisherman's hand.

What did he do then? What do you think? He jumped, seized the bundle between his teeth and, holding it carefully, ran out of the cave and away like lightning.

The fisherman was terribly angry to see the fish he had so badly wanted to eat, snatched from him, and he ran after the dog; but he had run only a few steps when he had a violent fit of coughing, and had to go back.

When Alidoro came to the road leading to the village, he stopped, and placed Pinocchio gently on the ground.

'How can I thank you?' said the puppet.

'No need to thank me,' answered the dog. 'You saved my life, and such a good turn deserves another. You know we must all help each other in this world.'

'How did you come to the cave?'

'I was lying on the sand more dead than alive, when the wind brought me the odour of fried fish. An odour such as that gave me an appetite, and I followed it. If I had been later . . .'

'Don't speak of it!' yelled Pinocchio, who was still trembling with fear. 'Don't mention it! If you had been later, I'd already have been fried, and eaten, and digested. B-r-r-r! It makes me shiver, just to think of it!'

Alidoro laughed, and held out his right paw to the puppet, who shook it heartily, as a sign of friendship, and then they parted.

The dog went home; but Pinocchio, when he was left alone, went to a little house near by, where an old man was sitting at the door, and said, 'Tell me, good old man, do you know anything about a poor boy, Eugene, who was wounded on the head?'

'Some fishermen carried him to this house, but now . . .'

'Now he is dead!' interrupted Pinocchio, sadly.

'No, he is alive, and went home.'

'Really? Truly?' cried the puppet, jumping for joy. 'So, then, his wound wasn't serious?'

'It might have been very serious; it might have killed him,' answered the old man, 'for they threw a heavy bound book at his head.'

'Who threw it?'

'One of his schoolmates, a certain Pinocchio.'

'Who is this Pinocchio?' inquired the puppet, as if he had never heard of him.

'They say he's a very bad boy, a vagabond, and a perfect good-for-nothing.'

'Slander! Pure slander!'

'Do you know this Pinocchio?'

'I know him by sight,' replied the puppet.

'And what do you think of him?' asked the old man.

'I think he is a very good boy, eager to study; he is obedient, and loves his father and his family.'

While telling all these fibs, the puppet touched his nose and, seeing that it had grown several inches, he grew very frightened, and cried, 'No, no, don't believe what I have said! I know Pinocchio very well, and can assure you he's a very bad boy. He is idle, and disobedient, and instead of going to school he amuses himself in the society of evil companions.'

As soon as he had said this, his nose grew shorter, as short as it was to begin with.

'Why are you so white' asked the old man suddenly.

'I'll tell you. Without noticing it, I rubbed myself against a wall that had just been whitewashed,' answered the puppet, for he was ashamed to confess that he had been floured like a fish, prepared for being fried.

'But what happened to your jacket, and your trousers, and your cap?'

'I met with thieves, and they robbed me of my clothes. Do you happen to have some old clothes you could give me? Then I could go home.'

'My child, I have nothing but a little bag in which I keep beans; if you want to have it, take it. You are welcome to it.'

There was no need to ask Pinocchio twice. He took the little bag and, cutting one hole in the bottom, with the scissors, and one on each side for his arms, he put it on like a shirt. And, in that rough garb, he started for home.

But as he went he began to feel very uncomfortable. He took one step forward, and then one backward, saying to himself, 'How can I ever approach that kind fairy? What will she say when she sees me? Will she forgive this second naughtiness? I don't think she will. Oh, I'm sure she won't. And it serves me right, for I am a wicked boy – always promising to better myself, and never keeping my word.'

It was night when he reached that village and very dark. As it was a stormy night, and was raining heavily, he went direct to the fairy's house, resolved to knock at the door, knowing he would be let in.

But when he came to the door he was frightened to knock, and ran back some distance. He came to the door a second time, but could not make a final decision; a third time – it was just the same. The fourth time he seized the iron knocker and, trembling, let it fall very lightly.

He waited, and waited, and at last, after waiting half an hour, a window was opened on the top floor (the house had four floors) and a big snail with a tiny light on her head looked out, and said, 'Who is there, at this hour?'

'Is the fairy at home?' asked the puppet.

'The fairy is asleep and you mustn't disturb her. But who are you?'

'I am I.'

'I? who is I?'

'Pinocchio.'

'Who is Pinocchio?'

'The puppet who lives with the fairy.'

'Ah, I see!' said the snail. 'Wait for me. I'll come down at once, and open the door.'

'Hurry, for pity's sake! I am dying of cold.'

'My lad, I am a snail, and snails are never in a hurry.'

An hour passed; then two hours, but the door was not opened. Pinocchio, who was wet and shivering with cold and fright, gathered all his courage and knocked again, a little louder.

At this a window opened on the third floor, and the same snail looked out.

'Dear little snail,' cried Pinocchio from the street, 'I have been waiting two hours! And two hours in this awful weather seems longer than two years. Hurry up, for Heaven's sake!'

'My lad,' said the sluggish, calm snail, 'my lad, I am a snail, and snails are never in a hurry.' And the window was closed.

Not long after, the clock struck midnight; then one o'clock, two o'clock; but the door was still closed.

At last Pinocchio lost his patience. In a rage, he seized the knocker to strike a blow that would shake the whole house; but suddenly the iron knocker turned into an eel and, slipping out of his hands, disappeared in the stream that was running in the street.

'Oh – ho!' shouted Pinocchio, blind with rage. 'If the knocker can run away, I can kick the door.'

And drawing back, he gave a huge kick against the door. He kicked so hard that his foot went through the wood and, when he tried to pull it back, he couldn't. His foot was embedded in the door as firmly as a nail driven by a hammer.

Imagine poor Pinocchio! He had to spend the rest of the night with one foot on the ground, and the other in the door.

Finally, at dawn the door was opened. That kind snail had spent only nine hours coming down from the fourth storey to the door. She must have been in a terrible hurry!

'What are you doing there, with your foot in the door?' she asked, laughing.

'It was an accident. Won't you try, kind snail, to free me from this trouble?'

'My lad, this is a job for a carpenter, and I have never been a carpenter.'

'Beg the fairy to help me.'

'The fairy is sleeping, and mustn't be disturbed.'

'But what can I do all day, stuck to this door?'

'You can amuse yourself counting the ants that are passing by.'

'At least bring me something to eat, for I am terribly hungry.'

'At once!' said the snail.

In fact, three and a half hours later Pinocchio saw her coming back with a silver tray on her head, holding some bread, a roast chicken, and four ripe apricots.

'Here is the breakfast the fairy sends you,' said the snail.

Seeing all those good things, the puppet was quite relieved. But how disappointed he grew when he discovered that the bread was plaster, the chicken made of board, and the four apricots coloured alabaster.

He wanted to cry, and, in his despair, he tried to throw away the tray and all that was on it; but instead, owing to his grief and his great weakness, he fainted.

When he came to himself, he was lying on a sofa, and the fairy was beside him.

'I shall forgive you once more,' said the fairy; 'but never more if you misbehave again.'

Pinocchio vowed and promised that he would study, and always be good; and he kept his word for the rest of the year. He was first in the examinations, and became the best scholar in the school. His conduct was so satisfactory and praiseworthy, that the fairy was very pleased, and said, 'Tomorrow your wish shall be granted.'

'Do you mean . . .?'

'Tomorrow you shall cease to be a wooden puppet, and become a real boy.'

No one, without seeing Pinocchio at the moment he

heard this longed-for news, can imagine his joy. All his classmates were invited to the fairy's house the next day, for a grand breakfast to celebrate the important event. The fairy prepared two hundred cups of coffee with cream, and four hundred bread rolls, buttered on both sides. The day promised to be a most happy and pleasant one, but . . .

Most unfortunately, in the lives of puppets there is always a '*but*' that spoils everything.

CHAPTER 30

Pinocchio listens to his friend Lampwick,
who is going to Playland

As one would expect, Pinocchio asked permission from the fairy to go to the village and invite his friends for the next day.

The fairy said, 'Yes, by all means, go and invite your friends for breakfast, but remember to be back before dark. Do you understand?'

'I promise to be back in an hour,' said the puppet.

'Be careful, Pinocchio. Children make promises very easily, but they are not so ready to keep their promises.'

'But I'm different from other children; when I say a thing, I do it.'

'We shall see. This time, if you are disobedient, so much the worse for you.'

'Why?'

'Because children who do not follow the advice of those who are wiser than they are, always come to grief.'

'But I have learnt my lesson!' said Pinocchio. 'And I shall never blunder again.'

'We shall see if that's true.'

The puppet said not a word more, kissed the good fairy, who was like a mother to him, and ran out of the house singing and dancing.

In less than an hour he had invited all his friends. Some of them accepted at once, with pleasure. Others waited to be urged; but when they heard that the rolls, which were to be dipped in the coffee and milk, would be buttered on both sides, they all said, 'Yes, we'll come too, to please you.'

Now you must know that Pinocchio had, among his schoolmates, one favourite of whom he was very fond. His name was Romeo, but everybody called him by his nickname, Lampwick, because he was so thin, long, and bright, just like a new wick on a night-lamp.

Lampwick was the laziest and most mischievous boy in the school, but Pinocchio liked him none the less. In fact, he went to him first of all, but he was not at home. He went back a second time, but no Lampwick; a third time, but still in vain.

Where could he be? He searched for him everywhere, and finally he found him hiding under the porch of a peasant's house.

'What are you doing there?' asked Pinocchio, creeping under the porch.

'I'm waiting for midnight, when I'm going . . .'

'Where are you going?'

'Far, very far away.'

'I went to your place three times looking for you.'

'What do you want with me?'

'Have you not heard the great news? Don't you know of my good fortune?'

'What?'

'From tomorrow I shall no longer be a puppet but a boy like you, and the other boys.'

'Much good may it do you!'

'And tomorrow I expect you at my house for breakfast.'

'But didn't I tell you that I'm going away tonight?'

'At what time?'

'At midnight.'

'Where are you going?'

'I'm going to live in a country – the most beautiful country in the world – a real dreamland.'

'What's its name?'

'It's called Playland. Why don't you come too?'

'I? Certainly not!'

'You are wrong, Pinocchio! Believe me, if you don't come, you will be sorry. Where could you find a better place for us boys? There's no school there, no masters, and no books. In that heavenly place, no one ever studies. There's no school on Saturday; and in every week there are six Saturdays, and one Sunday. Just imagine! The autumn holidays begin in January, and last till the thirty-first of December. Now, a place like that is the ideal place to live in! That's how all civilized countries should be run.'

'But how do they pass the time in Playland?'

'How? Play and amuse themselves from morning till night. Then they go to bed, and start again next morning. What do you think of that?'

'Um!' said Pinocchio, and shook his head as if to say, 'That sort of life wouldn't be too bad!'

'Now then, will you come, or won't you? Yes, or no? Make up your mind!'

'No, no, no, and finally no! I promised the good fairy to be a good boy, and I must keep my promise. In fact, it's nearly evening, so I must leave you and hurry back. Good-bye, and a pleasant journey!'

'Where are you going in such a hurry?'

'I'm going home. The good fairy wants me to be home before dark.'

'Wait a little longer.'

'I shall be too late.'

'Just two minutes.'

'And if the fairy scolds me?'

'Let her scold. When she's done scolding, she'll stop,' said that rascal of a Lampwick.

'How are you going? Alone, or in company?'

'Alone? There'll be more than a hundred boys with me!'

'Are you going on foot?'

'A stagecoach is coming soon to take us to that dream country.'

'What wouldn't I give if the coach were coming right now!'

'Why?'

'Because I could see you all starting together.'

'Stay a little longer, and you can do so.'

'No, no, I must go.'

'Wait just two more minutes.'

'I've waited too long already. The fairy won't know what's happened to me.'

'Poor fairy! Is she afraid the bats will eat you?'

'No, no. But . . .' continued Pinocchio, 'are you absolutely sure there are no schools in that country?'

'Not a single one!'

'And no masters?'

'Not one.'

'And no one ever has to study?'

'Never, never, never!'

'What a beautiful country!' sighed Pinocchio. 'Of course I've never been there, but I can imagine what it must be like.'

'Why don't you come, then?'

'It's useless to tempt me. I've promised the good fairy to be an obedient boy, and I shall not break my word.'

'Well, good-bye then, and give my love to the boys at the schools – and to all the high schools, too, if you meet them on the street.'

'Good-bye, Lampwick. I wish you a pleasant journey. I hope you'll have a fine time, and think of your friends now and then.'

Saying this the puppet took a few steps but then stopped and, turning to his friend, he asked, 'Are you quite sure that there are six Saturdays and one Sunday in a week?'

'Quite.'

'Are you sure, but really sure that holidays begin on the first of January, and end on the thirty-first of December?'

'Perfectly sure.'

'What a wonderful country!' said Pinocchio again, delightedly. Then he added quickly with a final resolution, 'Well, good-bye, and I hope you have a good journey!'

'Good-bye.'

'How long before you start?'

'A little over an hour.'

'A pity! If it were only one hour, I could perhaps be tempted to wait and see you off.'

'And the fairy?'

'I've waited so long already, an hour more or less wouldn't matter.'

'Poor Pinocchio! And if the fairy scolds you?'

'Never mind! I'd let her scold. When she's done scolding she'll stop.'

Meanwhile, it grew very dark. Suddenly they saw a little light moving, in the distance, and heard bells tinkling, people talking and the hooting of a horn, very faint and low, like the humming of a wasp.

'There it is!' exclaimed Lampwick, jumping to his feet.

'What is it?' Pinocchio asked softly.

'It's the coach coming for me. Do you want to come too? Yes, or no?'

'But is it true,' asked the puppet, 'that children never have to study in that country?'

'Never, never, never!'

'What a wonderful country! What a beautiful country! What a marvellous country!'

CHAPTER 31

Pinocchio goes away to Playland, where he spends five months

At last the coach arrived, without making the least noise, for the wheels were padded with rags and tow.

It was drawn by twelve pairs of donkeys, all the same size, but of different colours. Some were grey, some white, some spotted, others again were yellow and blue in large stripes.

But the funniest thing about them was that these twelve pairs, that is twenty-four donkeys, were not shod like other animals; they had on men's boots of white leather.

And the driver?

Imagine a small man broader than he is long, soft and greasy as butter, with a small face like a red tomato, a little mouth that is always laughing, and a soft, caressing voice, like that of a cat that is mewing to the lady of the house for cream.

All the boys took a great fancy to him as soon as they saw him; and they all hurried to get in first, and go to that most delightful country known on the map as True Playland.

The coach was already full of boys between eight and twelve years old, pressed together like salted fish in a barrel. They were crowded and uncomfortable, and they could hardly breathe, but no one said a word. No one complained. The consolation of knowing that in a few hours they would be in a land where there were no books, or schools, or masters, made them accept anything; and they were so happy that they did not feel discomfort, weariness, hunger, thirst, or sleepiness.

As soon as the coach stopped, the little man turned to Lampwick and, with many bows and grimaces, said to him, smiling, 'Tell me, my fine lad, would you also like to go to that happy country?'

'I want to go, most certainly.'

'But as you see, my dear lad, there is no room; the coach is full.'

'It doesn't matter,' replied Lampwick. 'If there's no room inside, I'll find some place on the crossbar.' And he jumped up astride the crossbar.

'And you, my love,' said the little man, addressing Pinocchio, with a flattering smile, 'what are you going to do? Are you coming or staying behind?'

'I'm staying here,' answered Pinocchio, 'for I am going home. I want to study and be a very good scholar, like all well-brought-up boys.'

'Much good may it do you!'

'Pinocchio,' cried Lampwick, 'listen to me! Come with us! We'll have a marvellous time.'

'No, no, no!'

'Come with us! We'll have lots of fun!' shouted some voices inside the coach.

'Come with us! We'll all be happy!' shouted hundreds of voices together.

'If I come with you, what would my good fairy say?' continued Pinocchio.

'Don't worry about that. Think only that we are going to a country where we'll have nothing but fun from morning till night.'

Pinocchio did not answer; he only sighed. He sighed a second time, a third time, and at last he said, 'Make a little room for me. I am coming.'

'Everything is full,' replied the little man, 'but to show you how happy I am that you're with us, I shall give you my place.'

'And what will you do?'

'I shall walk.'

'No, I can't let you do that. I'd rather ride on one of the donkeys!' cried Pinocchio.

So saying, he went up to the donkey harnessed to the right-hand side of the shaft, and wanted to jump on his back, but the beast turned and kicked him in the stomach, sending him sprawling with his legs in the air.

Think of all those impertinent boys, nearly bursting with laughter.

But the little man did not laugh. He went to that kicking donkey and, pretending to give him a kiss, he bit off half his right ear.

While he was doing this Pinocchio, still angry, got up from the ground and, with one leap, jumped on the donkey's back. He jumped so splendidly that all the boys stopped laughing, and shouted, 'Hurrah, Pinocchio!' and applauded as if they would never stop.

But suddenly the donkey kicked so high with his hind legs that he threw the poor puppet on to a heap of stones.

The boys laughed at him again; but the little man, instead of laughing, went to the other side of the kicking beast, and bit off half of his left ear.

Then he told the puppet, 'Now get on his back. You needn't be frightened. That donkey is very obstinate but I've whispered something in his ear, and I think he'll be obedient and gentle now.'

Pinocchio mounted again, and the coach started to move; but while the donkeys galloped and the coach rolled over the paving stones, he thought he heard a voice which was so low that he could hardly hear the words, saying, 'You poor fool! You decided to do as you please, but you'll be sorry for it!'

Pinocchio was frightened, and looked around to see where these words came from, but he could see nothing. The donkeys galloped, the stagecoach rolled over the stones, and the boys inside slept. Lampwick snored like a bear; and the little man sang between his teeth,

> *Everybody sleeps through the night*
> *while I never sleep . . .*

A little way farther on Pinocchio heard again the low voice saying, 'Remember this, you fool – boys who won't study, and who desert their school, their books, and their masters, always come to a bad end. I have tried it, and I know what I am talking about. The day will come when you will weep as I am weeping now; but then it will be too late!'

When he heard these whispered words, the puppet was more frightened than ever. He jumped down from the donkey's back, and took him by the bridle.

Imagine his surprise when he saw that the donkey was crying, just like a boy.

'Hullo, little man,' Pinocchio called the driver. 'Did you ever see such a thing? This donkey is crying.'

'Let him cry! He can laugh on Tib's Eve.'

'Did you teach him to talk?'

'No, he taught himself to mumble a few words when he was in a company of trained dogs for three years.'

'Poor beast!'

'Come, come!' said the little man. 'Don't waste time watching a donkey cry. Get on to him again, and let us go! The night is cold and the way is long.'

Pinocchio obeyed without another word. The coach rolled along again, and at dawn they arrived safely at Playland.

Playland was like no other country in the world. The population consisted of children. The eldest was fourteen, and the youngest scarcely eight years old. The merriment and shouting and noise in the streets were maddening.

There were children everywhere. Some were playing skittles, some quoits, cycling or ball, some were riding on wooden horses; others were playing blind-man's buff, or chasings; some were dressed as clowns, and were eating burning tow; some were acting, or singing, or reading, or turning somersaults; others were walking on their hands, while still others were trundling hoops or, dressed like generals, were marching along with paper helmets ordering troops of soldiers about. There was laughing, and shouting, and hand-clapping; some were whistling; some were clucking like a hen that has just laid an egg. In short, there was such noise and confusion that, without cotton wool in both ears, anyone would have been deafened by it. There were theatres, crowded all day long, in every open space, and on all the walls of the houses, badly spelt remarks had been scribbled with charcoal.

Immediately they got inside the city, Lampwick, and the other boys who had come together, hurried to join the children, and very soon, as you may well imagine, they became excellent friends. Who could be happier, or more contented, than they?

Amidst continual games and all sorts of pastimes, hours, days and weeks passed like lightning.

'Oh, what a beautiful life!' shouted Pinocchio, every time he met Lampwick.

'Do you at last see that I was right?' answered Lampwick. 'And to think you didn't want to come! To think you intended going back to your fairy, and wasting your time in studying! If you are free today from nasty books and schools, you owe it to me, to my advice, to my insistence. It's only a real friend who would show such kindness.'

'Yes, that's true, Lampwick! If today I am a really happy

boy, I owe it all to you. And do you know what the master used to say to me about you? He always said, "Don't have anything to do with that good-for-nothing Lampwick. He is a very bad boy, and will lead you into some trouble."'

'Poor old master!' said the other, shaking his head. 'I well know that he didn't like me, and spoke ill of me. But I have a generous soul, and with pleasure I forgive him.'

'Noble boy!' said Pinocchio, embracing his friend, and kissing him affectionately on the forehead.

Five months had passed in this playland, of toys and amusements which went on all day long, without ever seeing a book or even the outside of a school, when Pinocchio, upon awaking one morning, had a very unpleasant surprise, and lost his good spirits.

CHAPTER 32

Pinocchio gets donkey's ears, and then
becomes a real donkey and starts to bray

And what was this surprise?

I shall tell you, my dear readers. The surprise was that Pinocchio, when he woke up, scratched his head; and while doing so he noticed . . .

Can you make any guess as to what he noticed?

He noticed, to his great amazement, that his ears had grown several inches.

You must know that puppets from their birth have very small ears; in fact so small that they are invisible to the naked eye. So you can imagine how surprised he was when he noticed that his ears had grown so long during the night that they looked like two brooms.

He hurried to find a mirror, that he might see himself; but he could not find one. So he filled his wash basin with water, looked into it, and saw what he had been hoping never to see. He saw himself decorated with a magnificent pair of donkey's ears.

Can you imagine poor Pinocchio's sorrow, shame, and despair?

He began to cry, and scream, and beat his head against

the wall; but the more he cried, the longer his ears grew, and they became hairy at the top.

A charming little squirrel that lived on the floor above him, hearing his loud cries, came down to see what the matter was; and, seeing the puppet in such a state, she asked earnestly, 'What's happened to you, my dear neighbour?'

'I am sick, dear squirrel, I am very sick – and of such an awful disease. Do you know how to count a pulse?'

'Yes, I think so.'

'Then will you please see if I have a fever?'

The squirrel put her right forepaw on Pinocchio's pulse, and then said with a sigh, 'My friend, I am very sorry, but I have bad news for you.'

'What is it?'

'You have a very dangerous fever.'

'What kind of fever is it?'

'Donkey fever.'

'I never heard of such a fever!' said the puppet, though he knew well what she meant.

'Then I shall explain it to you,' answered the squirrel, 'for you must know that in a few hours you will no longer be a puppet, or a boy . . .'

'What will I be?'

'In a few hours you will be a real donkey, like those that draw carts, or carry cabbages and vegetables to the market.'

'Oh, poor me! Poor me!' cried Pinocchio, seizing his ears with his hands, and pulling and jerking them, as if they belonged to somebody else.

'My dear lad,' said the squirrel, wishing to console him, 'you can't do anything. It is your destiny. For it is written in the decrees above that lazy children who dislike books, schools, and masters, and who spend their time with toys, games, and amusements, must end up, sooner or later, by becoming little donkeys.'

'Is that really true?' sobbed Pinocchio.

'It is, unhappily. It's no use crying now. You should have thought of that before it was too late.'

'But it's not my fault. Believe me, little squirrel, it's all Lampwick's fault!'

'Who is Lampwick?'

'One of my schoolmates. I wanted to go home; I wanted to be good; I wanted to study and never do any mischief; but Lampwick said, "Why should you bother about studying? Why do you want to go to school? Instead, come with me to Playland. There we shall never study; we shall only play from morning till evening, and always be happy!"'

'Why did you listen to that false friend – to that bad companion?'

'Because . . . because, dear little squirrel, I am a heartless puppet, with no sense. Oh, if I had just a little bit of heart, I'd never have abandoned that kind fairy who loved me as a mother, and who had done so much for me! And now I could be a real boy, like the others, instead of a puppet! Oh, if I meet Lampwick, he'll get it! I'll fix him!'

He wanted to leave the room, but at the door he remembered his ears, and he was ashamed to show them. So then what do you think he did? He took a large cotton cap, and pulled it over his head, right down to his nose.

Then he went out, and looked for Lampwick. He searched the streets, the squares, and theatres, everywhere, but he could not find him. He turned to everyone he met, but no one had seen him. At last he went to his house and knocked at the door.

'Who's there?' asked Lampwick, from inside.

'Pinocchio,' said the puppet.

'Just a minute, and I'll let you in.'

After half an hour the door was opened. Imagine Pinocchio's surprise, when he went in and found that his friend Lampwick had a great cotton cap on his head which came down over the end of his nose.

Seeing that, Pinocchio felt somewhat better, and he said to himself, 'Perhaps he has the same sickness as I have. Can it be possible that he, too, has the donkey fever?'

He pretended not to see anything, and said, smiling, 'How are you, my dear Lampwick?'

'Very well. As well as a mouse in a Parmesan cheese.'

'Do you really mean it?'

'I have no reason to tell you a lie.'

'Excuse me, my friend, but why then do you wear a cap that covers your ears?'

'The doctor ordered it, because I've hurt my knee. And you, dear puppet, why do you wear a cotton cap down over your nose?'

'The doctor prescribed it, because I hurt my leg.'

'Oh, poor Pinocchio!'

'Oh, poor Lampwick!'

They kept silent for a long while and the two friends looked knowingly at each other.

At last the puppet said, in a sweet voice full of persuasion, 'Just to satisfy my curiosity, dear Lampwick, have you ever had any trouble with your ears?'

'Never! And you?'

'Never! Except that one of my ears was aching this morning.'

'Yes, so was mine.'

'Yours, too? Which one aches?'

'Both of them. And yours?'

'Both of them. Do you think we have the same sickness?'

'I'm afraid I do.'

'Will you do me a favour, Lampwick?'

'Yes, with the greatest pleasure.'

'Will you let me see your ears?'

'Why not? But first I'd like to see yours, dear Pinocchio.'

'No, you be the first.'

'No, dear fellow. You first, and then I'll show mine.'

'Well,' said the puppet, 'let us agree, like good friends.'

'What to?'

'We'll take off our caps at the same time. Agreed?'

'Agreed.'

'Then, ready!' And Pinocchio begun to count in a loud voice, 'One! Two! Three!'

At 'Three!' they took off their caps, and threw them in the air.

And then something happened that sounds unbelievable, yet it was true. When Pinocchio and Lampwick saw that the same misfortune had befallen them both, instead of being ashamed and despairing, they tried to wag their long ears, and finished by laughing at each other.

They laughed and laughed, until they nearly exploded.

But suddenly Lampwick stopped laughing. He staggered and grew pale as he spoke to his friend, 'Help, help, Pinocchio!'

'What's the trouble?'

'Alas! I can't stand up straight.'

'Neither can I,' cried Pinocchio, tottering and weeping.

While talking they bent down on all fours, and started running round the room on their hands and feet. As they ran, their hands became hoofs, their faces grew as long as muzzles, and their backs were covered by light grey hair with black spots.

But the most dreadful and the most humiliating moment for those two miserable boys was when they felt their tails growing. Overcome by shame and sorrow, they began to cry, and lament over their fate.

Oh, if they had only kept quiet! Instead of sighs and lamentations, they brayed like donkeys. Yes, both together, in chorus, they brayed loudly.

Meanwhile somebody knocked at the door, and a voice shouted, 'Open the door! I am the little man, the driver who brought you here. Open at once, or it will be the worse for you!'

CHAPTER 33

As Pinocchio becomes a real donkey, he is sold to the manager of a show and learns how to dance and jump through a hoop; but he is lamed one evening, and then is bought by a man who decides to make a drum of his skin

As they did not open the door, the little man kicked it open, and addressed Pinocchio and Lampwick with his usual laugh.

'Hurrah for you! You brayed very well; I recognized your voices at once. And now, here I am.'

At these words the two donkeys became silent, their heads were hanging down, and their tails between their legs.

At first the little man stroked and patted them; then drawing forth a curry-comb, he combed them well. When they were shiny so that he could see his face in them, he bridled them, and took them to market, hoping to sell them at a profit.

Indeed, buyers were not lacking. Lampwick was sold to a farmer whose donkey had died the day before; and Pinocchio was bought by the manager of a company of clowns and rope-walkers, who intended teaching him to jump and dance, together with the other animals belonging to the company.

Now you can see, my little readers, what a fine business

the little man carried on? He was a cruel little monster, seemingly all milk and honey, going round the world with his coach. By promises and flattery he collected all the children who did not like their books, and did not want to go to school. When his coach was full he carried the children off to Playland, so that they might spend their time playing and amusing themselves. When these poor children, from endless playing and lack of studying, became so many donkeys, he took them to market and sold them happily. In a few years, by this means, he earned a lot of money, and became a millionaire.

I do not know what happened to Lampwick, but I know that Pinocchio, from the very first moment, led a hard life full of drudgery.

When he was led into the stable, his master put straw in his manger, but Pinocchio spat it out after he had tasted it.

Then his master, grumbling, put some hay in the manger; but Pinocchio did not like that either.

'Ah! You don't even like hay?' shouted his master, full of anger. 'Leave it to me, my fine donkey! If you are so fussy, I know how to cure you!' And he beat his legs with his whip for a start.

The pain made Pinocchio cry, and bray, 'Ee-a! I can't digest straw!'

'Then eat hay,' replied his master, who understood donkey dialect perfectly.

'Ee-a! Hay gives me the stomach ache!'

'Do you want to tell me I have to feed a donkey like you on chicken breasts and capon jelly?' said his master, growing still more angry, whipping him again and again.

After this second whipping Pinocchio thought it would be wiser to keep silent, and he said no more. The stable door was shut, and Pinocchio remained alone. As it was so long since he had eaten anything, hunger made him yawn; and when he yawned he opened his mouth as large as an oven.

At last, as there was nothing but hay in his manger, he decided to eat it, and after chewing it a long time, he shut his eyes and swallowed it.

'This hay isn't so bad,' he said. 'But how much better it would have been if I'd gone on with my studies! Instead of hay, I might now be eating the crusty end of a fresh loaf of bread, with a fine slice of sausage! No matter!'

In the morning, he looked again for a little hay; but he found none, for he had eaten it all during the night.

Then he tried a mouthful of chopped straw, but as he chewed it he thought what a difference there was between the taste of chopped straw, and rice, or macaroni.

'No matter!' he said again, as he went on chewing. 'I hope my misfortune will serve as a lesson to disobedient children who don't like studying. No matter! No matter!'

'Why "No matter"?' shouted his master, who came into the stable at that moment. 'Do you think, my dear donkey, that I bought you just to feed? I bought you to do some work, and to help me make money. Get up, now, and do your best! Come into the circus, and I'll teach you to jump through a hoop, breaking the paper with your head; to dance, waltz and polka, and to stand on your hind legs.'

So poor Pinocchio, by hook or by crook, had to learn all these fine tricks; but it took him three months, and he got many sharp cuts from the whip.

At last the day arrived when his master announced a really wonderful performance. Gaily coloured posters were placed at all the street corners.

You may believe me the theatre was full an hour before the opening of the show.

Not one more seat could have been bought, even for its weight in gold. The seats round the ring were packed with girls and boys, impatient to see the famous little donkey Pinocchio dancing.

After the first part of the show, the ringmaster came

forward. He was wearing a black coat, with white tights and boots reaching above his knees. After a deep bow, he made the following ridiculous speech:

'Honoured public, ladies and gentlemen!

'The humble undersigned staying temporarily in your city, wishes to have the honour, not less than the pleasure, of presenting to this intelligent and distinguished audience a famous little donkey, who has had the honour of dancing before the sovereigns of all the principal courts of Europe.

'I thank you for listening attentively to me, and beg that you assist us with your inspiring presence, and find excuses for our shortcomings.'

This speech was received with much laughter and applause; but the applause redoubled, and became tempestuous, when the Little Donkey Pinocchio appeared in the middle of the ring. He was magnificently decked out! He had a new bridle of shiny leather, with brass buckles and studs, and white camellias behind his ears. His mane was divided into small curls, each one decorated with coloured silk ribbons, a broad band of gold and silver surrounded his body, and his tail was braided with crimson and blue velvet ribbons. In fact, he was a lovely little donkey.

Presenting him to the public the manager added these words: 'Honourable audience! I am not here to tell you untrue stories about the great difficulties I had to conquer in order to capture and subjugate this mammal, as he was feeding, wild and free, in the mountains and plains of the torrid zone. Observe, I beseech you, the ferocious gleams in his eyes. After every tender means of taming him failed, I was forced to use the last resort, the whip. Yet all my kindness, which should have increased his love for me, only made him fiercer day by day. However, following the system of Gall, I found on his cranium a bump, which the Faculty of Medicine in Paris declared to be the generator of hair and of dance. Therefore, I have taught him to dance, and also to jump through hoops and frames covered with paper. Admire him, and judge him! But before I take my leave of you, permit me, ladies and gents, to invite you to the performance of tomorrow evening. Should bad weather threaten, then the show, instead of tomorrow evening, will be set back to tomorrow, at eleven o'clock in the a.m.'

Here the ringmaster bowed again and then, turning to Pinocchio, he said, 'Come, Pinocchio! Before you start your performance, salute this distinguished audience – ladies, gentlemen, and children!'

Pinocchio obediently bent his knees, and remained kneeling until the ringmaster cracked his whip, and shouted, 'Walk!'

Then the little donkey got up and walked round the ring.

After a while the ringmaster shouted, 'Trot!' Pinocchio obeyed the order, and started to trot.

'Gallop!'

And Pinocchio broke into a gallop.

'Run!'

And Pinocchio ran as fast as he could.

Suddenly, while he raced round the ring, the ringmaster raised his arm in the air and fired off a pistol.

At that the donkey, pretending to be wounded, fell down as if he were dead.

As he rose up, amid applause and clapping of hands, he lifted his head and looked up at the people; and there he saw, in one of the boxes, a beautiful lady who wore a heavy gold chain round her neck, from which hung a medallion. On the medallion was the portrait of a puppet.

'That is my portrait! The lady is the fairy!' said Pinocchio to himself, recognizing her immediately.

He was so overcome with joy that he tried to cry, 'Oh, my dear fairy! Oh, my dear fairy!' But instead of these words, there came forth from his throat a bray – so long and loud that everyone present laughed, and especially the children.

Then the ringmaster to teach him that it was not good manners to bray like that before the public, struck him on the nose with the handle of his whip.

The poor little donkey put out his tongue, and licked his nose at least five minutes to ease the pain he felt.

But how great was his disappointment when, turning to the box again, he saw that it was empty. The fairy had disappeared!

He thought he was going to die; his eyes were full of tears and he began to cry bitterly.

However, no one noticed it; least of all the ringmaster, who, cracking his whip, shouted, 'Courage, Pinocchio! Now show this gracious audience how elegantly you can leap through the hoop.'

Pinocchio tried two or three times; but each time he came to the hoop, he thought it easier to run under, than through it. At last he leaped through it but his right hind-leg caught in the hoop, and he fell heavily to the ground on the other side.

When he got up he was lame, and could walk back to the stable only with great difficulty.

'Bring out Pinocchio! We want the little donkey! Bring out the little donkey!' shouted the children, who were all very sorry about his accident.

But the little donkey did not appear any more that evening.

When the veterinary surgeon – that is, the animal doctor – saw him the next morning, he declared that he would stay lame for the rest of his life.

Then the ringmaster said to his stable boy, 'What can I do with a lame donkey? Why should I feed him if he can't work? Take him to the market and sell him.'

As soon as they came to the market they found a buyer who asked the boy, 'How much do you want for this lame donkey?'

'Five crowns.'

'I'll give you fivepence. You mustn't think I'm buying him for use. I'm buying him only for his skin. I see he has a very hard skin and I want to make a drum for the village band.'

You can imagine how Pinocchio must have felt when he heard that he was to be a drum!

As soon as the fivepence was paid, the new owner led the little donkey to a rock by the shore, tied a stone to his neck, and a long rope to one leg. Then he gave him a sudden push, and Pinocchio fell into the water.

Pinocchio, with that stone on his neck, went immediately to the bottom; and his owner, holding the rope tight, sat down on the rock to wait until the donkey was drowned, so that he might skin him.

CHAPTER 34

Pinocchio, thrown into the sea and eaten by
the fishes, becomes a puppet again; but,
while swimming towards dry land, he is
swallowed by a terrible shark

When the little donkey had been underwater about an hour, his new owner said to himself, 'That poor little lame donkey must surely be drowned by this time! I'll pull him up, and make a fine drum of his skin.'

He began hauling in the rope he had tied to the donkey's leg. He hauled, and hauled, and hauled and at last there appeared on the water . . . what do you think? Instead of a dead donkey, there was a live puppet, wriggling like an eel.

When he saw that wooden puppet, the poor man thought he was dreaming. He was struck dumb and, astonished, he stood there with his mouth open, and his eyes starting out of his head.

When he recovered a little, he could only stammer, 'Where . . . where is the little donkey I threw into the water? What happened to him?'

'I am the little donkey!' answered the puppet, laughing.

'You!'

'I!'

'Ah, you scallywag, don't play any tricks on me!'

'Play tricks on you? Nothing of the sort, my dear master; I am very serious.'

'But how can it be that you, who were a little donkey a short while ago, have now become a wooden puppet?'

'It must be due to the sea water. It does, sometimes, work real miracles.'

'Be careful, puppet! Don't try to pull my leg! You'll get it if I lose my patience!'

'Well, master, do you want to hear my true story? If you free my leg from this rope, I'll tell it to you.'

The good man was very curious to hear his true story, so he quickly freed his leg, and Pinocchio, free as a bird once more, began to speak as follows:

'You must know that I was once a wooden puppet, just as I am now; and I was on the verge of becoming a real boy, like so many others. The trouble started because I didn't like to study, and I listened to evil companions, and so I ran away from home. One day I woke up to find myself a donkey, with long ears and a long tail. Oh, I was so ashamed of myself! Oh, dear master, I hope the good Saint Antony will keep you from ever being ashamed! I was taken to the market with the other donkeys, and sold to the ringmaster of a circus. He taught me to dance and leap through a hoop; but one evening, during the performance, I fell, and my legs got lamed. The ringmaster had no use for a lame donkey, so he sent me to the market, and you bought me.'

'I well know that, since I paid fivepence for you. And now, who will give me back my poor pennies?'

'And why did you buy me! To make a drum out of my skin! A drum!'

'That's true! And now where shall I find another skin?'

'Don't despair, master! There are so many little donkeys in this world.'

'Well, you impertinent urchin, is that the end of your story?'

'No,' answered the puppet. 'A couple more words, and I'll have finished. After buying me, you brought me here to kill me; and as you pitied me, you preferred to tie a stone to my neck, and throw me into the sea. This humane sentiment counts to your credit, and I shall be grateful to you for ever, my dear master. You reckoned without the fairy.'

'And who is this fairy?'

'She is my mother and, like every mother, she loves her child dearly, and never loses sight of him, and helps him in all his troubles, even when, because of his foolishness and his naughty ways, he deserves no help. So, as I wanted to say, as soon as the good fairy saw I was in danger of drowning she sent an immense shoal of fish who thought that I was a dead donkey, and began to eat me. And what huge bites they took! I would never have believed that fish were greedier than boys! Some ate my ears, others my muzzle, others my neck and mane, my hoofs, and even the skin off my leg and off my back; and one of them was so polite that he condescended to eat my tail.'

'From this day forward,' said this horrified buyer, 'I vow never to eat fish. It would be a pretty sight to open a mullet, or a whiting, and find a donkey's tail inside!'

'I agree with you,' said the puppet, laughing; 'as for that, you must know that when the donkey's hide that covered me from head to foot, was eaten away, naturally the bones remained – or, to be exact, the wood; for, as you see, I am made of very hard wood. But after the first bite, the fish saw that there was no more meat to eat and, disgusted by such indigestible food, they swam off in all directions, without even saying thank you. That is why, when you hauled in the rope, you found a live puppet and not a dead donkey.'

'Enough of your story!' shouted the man in a rage. 'I have paid fivepence for you, and I want my money back! Do you know what I'll do? I'll take you back to the market, and sell you for firewood.'

'Sell me if you want to. I don't mind,' said Pinocchio.

But as he spoke, he made a big leap, and plunged into the sea; and as he swam gaily away he shouted to the poor buyer, 'Good-bye, master! When you want a skin to make a drum, remember me.' He kept on laughing as he swam farther away.

After a little while he turned again, and shouted still louder, 'Good-bye, master! When you want a little nice dry firewood, remember me.'

In the twinkling of an eye he was so far away that he was hardly visible; in fact, there was only a black dot on the water when he now and then lifted an arm, or a leg, or jumped about like a joyful dolphin.

Pinocchio was swimming, not caring where he was going, when he saw in the sea a rock which looked like white marble. On the top of the rock a beautiful little goat was bleating, and beckoning to him to come nearer.

However, the strangest thing was, that the goat's fleece, instead of being white, or black, or a mixture of these two colours, as you find with other goats, was blue – a very bright blue, that reminded him of the hair of that lovely child.

Pinocchio's heart began to beat very quickly. Doubling his energy, he swam towards the white rock. He was already half-way there, when he saw, rushing towards him in the water, a sea monster with a horrible head, and its mouth, which was like a deep cave, wide open, with three rows of teeth that would have frightened anyone, even in a picture.

Do you know what this monster was?

It was no less than that gigantic shark, which has been mentioned more than once in this history, and which, owing to its dreadful killings and its ravenous greed, was called the 'Attila of fish and fishermen'.

Poor Pinocchio was terribly frightened seeing such a monster. He tried to dodge him, to swim elsewhere, or to swim faster than this monster; but that huge, gaping mouth came right after him, quickly as an arrow.

'Hurry, Pinocchio, for mercy's sake!' bleated the beautiful little goat.

Pinocchio swam desperately, using every ounce of his strength.

'Quickly, Pinocchio! The monster is close behind you!'

And Pinocchio swam faster than ever, swift as a ball from a gun. He was near the rock, and the little goat was leaning out over the sea, and stretching out her front legs to help him out of the water . . .

But it was too late! The monster had caught him and, drawing in his breath, he sucked him in as one sucks an egg. He sucked him in so fiercely and greedily, and Pinocchio fell so hard against the monster's stomach, that he lost consciousness for a quarter of an hour.

When he came to himself, he had no idea where he was. All around him it was very dark: the darkness was so thick and deep that he felt as if he had dived head first into a bottle full of ink. He listened, but he heard nothing: only from time to time, a great gust of wind blew in his face. At first he did not know where the wind came from, but he soon noticed that it came from the monster's lungs.

At first Pinocchio tried to be brave; but when he knew for certain that he was inside the shark's body, as in a prison, he began to weep and sob, 'Help! Help! Oh poor me! Will no one come and save me?'

'Who could come to save you, you miserable wretch?' said a voice in the darkness, like a guitar out of tune.

'Who speaks?' asked Pinocchio, frozen with fear.

'It's I. I'm a poor tunny fish, who was swallowed at the same time as you. What sort of a fish are you?'

'I have nothing to do with fishes. I'm a puppet.'

'If you're not a fish, why did you come here that the monster should swallow you?'

'I didn't *come* here; he swallowed me. What are we going to do now, in this cellar?'

'We must resign ourselves, and wait for the shark to digest us.'

'But I don't want to be digested!' shouted Pinocchio, beginning to cry again.

'Neither do I want to be digested!' said the tunny. 'But I'm wise enough to console myself with the thought that when one is born a tunny, it's more dignified to die in the water than in oil.'

'Stuff and nonsense!' cried Pinocchio.

'That is my opinion,' replied the tunny. 'And opinions, as our tunny politicians say, must be respected.'

'However that may be, I want to get away from here. I want to escape . . .'

'Escape then, if you can!'

'This shark that has swallowed us, is he very big?'

'His body is more than a mile long, and I'm not counting his tail.'

While they were talking in the darkness, Pinocchio thought he saw a gleam of light, very far away.

'What can that light be, that I see so far away?' asked Pinocchio.

'It's one of our fellows in misfortune, who, like us, is waiting to be digested.'

'I'm going to find him. It might possibly be an old fish who could tell me how to get out of here.'

'I hope so, dear puppet.'

'Good-bye, tunny.'

'Good-bye, puppet. Good luck to you.'

'Where shall we meet again?'

'Who knows? Better not to think of it.'

CHAPTER 35

*Pinocchio finds in the body of the shark . . .
whom does he find? Read this chapter, and
you will know*

Pinocchio, having said good-bye to the tunny, started feeling
his way in the darkness through the shark's body, finding his
way along, step by step, towards that dim, flickering light in
the distance.

The farther he went the better he could see the little
light. He walked and walked, and at last, when he reached
it, what did he find? I shall give you a thousand guesses. He
found a little table well prepared, with a lighted candle stuck
in a green glass bottle; and sitting at the table there was a
snow-white old man. He was eating some fish, which were
so much alive that sometimes they jumped out of his mouth
while he ate them.

Seeing the old man, poor Pinocchio suddenly felt so
happy that he nearly fainted. He wanted to laugh, to cry, to
say thousands of things; and instead he could only stammer
some broken, senseless words.

At last he managed to utter a cry of joy and, opening his
arms, he threw them around the old man's neck, shouting,
'Oh, Daddy! My Daddy! Have I found you at last? I'll never
leave you again – never, never, never!'

'So my eyes do not deceive me?' said the old man, rubbing them with both hands. 'You are really my dear Pinocchio?'

'Yes, yes, it's really, truly me! Do you still remember me? O, my dear Daddy, how good you are! And to think that I . . . Oh! but when you know how many things I've been through, and how many things have gone wrong . . . You know, dear Daddy, that the very same day you sold your coat to buy me a primer so that I could go to school, I ran away to see the puppet show; and the Showman was ready to put me in the fire, the better to roast his mutton. It was the same man who gave me five gold pieces to bring to you, but I met the fox and the cat, and they took me to the Red Crab Inn, where they gobbled up everything like hungry wolves, and I was left alone in the night. And I met assassins who ran after me, and I ran, and they followed me, and I ran, and they were still after me, and I ran until they hung me on a branch of the big oak tree, where the beautiful child with blue hair sent a carriage for me. And the doctors, when they looked at me, said straight away, "If he isn't dead, it shows that he's alive." And then I told a lie, and my nose began to grow, so that I couldn't get out of the room. And I went with the fox and the cat for the very purpose of burying the four gold pieces, for I'd spent one of them at the inn; and the parrot laughed at me, and instead of two thousand gold pieces I didn't find anything; and when the judge heard about it, he put me in jail to please the thieves. And when I left the prison, I saw a bunch of grapes, and I was caught in a trap; and the peasant, who was perfectly right, put a dog collar on me, and made me guard the poultry yard; but he soon found out I was innocent, and sent me away. And the serpent with the smoking tail started to laugh, and broke a blood vessel, and then I came back to the beautiful child's home, but she was dead, and the pigeon saw that I was crying, and said, "I saw your father making a boat to go after you," and I said, "Oh, if only I had wings, too!" and he said, "Do you want to go to your father?" and I said, "*Do* I? Of course I do! But who will take me?" and he said, "I will take you," and I said, "How?" and he said, "Get on my back." And so we flew all night, and when morning came we saw the fishermen looking out over the sea, and they said to me, "There's a poor man in a tiny boat, who'll soon be drowned." And I knew you at once, for though you were so far away, my heart told me it was you; and I made signs to you to come back . . .'

'I recognized you, too,' said Geppetto, 'and I would have been glad to come back, but how could I? The waves were so high, and a giant one upset my boat. A horrid shark that was near, came towards me as soon as he saw me in the water, and, sticking out his tongue, he swallowed me as if I had been a tart.'

'How long have you been shut up in here?' asked Pinocchio.

'It must surely be two years since that day – two years, my Pinocchio, that have seemed like two centuries.'

'How have you managed to live here? Where did you find the candle? And the matches to light it? Who gave them to you?'

'If you listen I'll tell you the whole story. In that same storm that overturned my boat, a merchant ship was also sunk. The sailors were all saved, but the ship was lost. The shark had a very good appetite that day, and after he had swallowed me, he swallowed the ship, too.'

'What! How did he do it?' asked Pinocchio in amazement.

'All in one mouthful. All that he spat out was the mainmast, because it stuck between his teeth, like a fish bone. Luckily for me, the ship was full of cans of preserved meat, biscuits, bottles of wine, dried grapes, cheese, coffee, sugar, candles, and matches. With all these provisions I have been able to live for two years; but now my supply is exhausted. There is nothing left in the pantry, and the candle you see is the last one.'

'And then?'

'And then, my dear, we shall remain in the dark.'

'Then, dear Daddy,' said Pinocchio, 'there is no time to lose. We must find a way to escape immediately.'

'To escape . . . But how?'

'We might escape through the mouth of the shark, into the sea, and swim away.'

'That's all very well, dear Pinocchio, but I can't swim.'

'That doesn't matter. I am a good swimmer. You can come on my back, and I'll carry you safely to the shore.'

'It's no use, my boy,' answered Geppetto, with a sad smile, shaking his head. 'A puppet like you, only three feet tall, could not be strong enough to swim if I were on his back.'

'Try it, and you'll see!'

Without another word, Pinocchio took the candle, went ahead and showed his father the way, saying to him, 'Follow me, and don't be frightened!'

They went like this for some time, through the whole body and the stomach of the shark. When they came to his throat, they stopped to look round, as they wanted to seize the right moment for their flight.

You must know that the shark was very old, and that as he suffered from asthma and palpitation of the heart, he had to sleep with his mouth wide open. So, when Pinocchio reached his throat and looked upwards, he could see a large strip of starry sky, and a big bright moon.

'This is the right moment to escape,' he whispered to his father. 'The shark is sleeping like a dormouse. The sea is smooth, and it is as bright as day. Come, Daddy – come after me, and in a few minutes we shall be free!'

And they did it. They climbed up the shark's throat, and when they were in that huge mouth they passed his tongue on tiptoe. His tongue was as long and wide as a fair-sized garden path. They were just prepared to jump into the sea when the shark sneezed, shaking them so violently that they fell back into his stomach.

Their fall extinguished the candle, and father and son were in the dark.

'Now what shall we do?' said Pinocchio.

'Now, my son, we are lost!'

'Why should we be lost? Give me your hand, Daddy, and be careful not to slip.'

'Where are we going?'

'We must try again. Come with me, and don't be frightened!'

With these words, Pinocchio took his father's hand, and, all the time walking on tiptoe, again they went up the monster's throat, walked along his tongue, and climbed over the three rows of teeth.

Before jumping into the sea the puppet said to his father, 'Now climb on my back, and stick tight. I'll do the rest.'

As soon as Geppetto was on his back, Pinocchio jumped into the sea and began to swim. The sea was as smooth as oil, the moon shone brightly and the shark slept so soundly that the firing of a cannon would not have disturbed him.

CHAPTER 36

At last Pinocchio ceases to be a puppet, and becomes a real boy

While Pinocchio was swimming towards the land as quickly as he could, he noticed that his father, sitting on his back with his legs in the water, was trembling violently, as though feverish.

Was he shivering because of cold, or of fright? Who knows? Perhaps a little of both. But Pinocchio thought he was frightened, and he tried to comfort him, 'Courage, Daddy! In a few minutes, we shall reach land, and be safe.'

'But where is this land?' asked the old man, growing more uneasy every moment, and blinking like a sailor threading a needle. 'Here I am looking everywhere, and I can't see anything but water and sky.'

'But I see land, too,' said the puppet. 'You know I am like a cat: I see better at night than in the daytime.'

Poor Pinocchio pretended to be cheerful, but he was rather discouraged. He grew weaker, and breathed with difficulty; in short he was almost exhausted, and land was still very far away.

He swam until he could breathe no longer: then he turned to his father, and said, 'Daddy, help me . . . I am dying!'

Father and son were about to drown together, when a voice, like a badly tuned guitar, said, 'Who is dying?'

'I, and my poor father!'

'I recognize your voice! You are Pinocchio!'

'Right. And who are you?'

'I am the tunny fish, your pal in the shark's body.'

'How did you escape?'

'I did the same as you, but you showed the way. I followed you, and I, too, escaped.'

'Dear tunny, you've come just in time! I beg you, for the love you have for your children, the little tunnies, to help us, or we are lost.'

'Of course! With all my heart. Catch my tail, and let me tow you. You will reach land in four minutes.'

You can be sure that Geppetto and Pinocchio accepted the invitation at once; but, instead of catching the tunny's tail, they found it better to sit on his back.

'Are we too heavy?' asked Pinocchio.

'Heavy! No, on the contrary, you're light as a feather! It's as if I had two empty seashells on my back,' answered the tunny, who was as big and strong as a two-year-old calf.

Reaching land, Pinocchio jumped down first, and then he helped his father. Then he turned to the tunny, and said in a trembling voice, 'My dearest friend, you have saved my father's life! I cannot find words to thank you. May I give you a kiss, as a token of my eternal gratitude?'

The tunny put his nose out of the water, and Pinocchio, kneeling on the ground, pressed a loving kiss on its mouth. At this sign of real, unaffected love, the tunny, who was not used to such things, was so moved that, ashamed to be seen crying like a baby, he dived under the water, and disappeared.

Meanwhile, the sun had risen.

Pinocchio gave his arm to Geppetto, who was so weak that he could hardly stand, and said, 'Lean on my arm, dear Daddy, and let us go. We must walk slowly, like snails; and when we are tired we shall stop and rest.'

'And where shall we go?' asked Geppetto.

'We'll try to find a house, or a cabin, where we can ask for a bit of bread, and some straw to make our bed.'

They had walked hardly a hundred steps when they noticed by the roadside two ugly faces, waiting to beg of the passers-by.

They were the fox and the cat, but they were so changed that you could hardly have recognized them. The cat had pretended so long to be blind that she really had become blind; the fox had grown old, his fur was entirely moth-eaten on one side, and he had even lost his tail. This had happened because the wretched thief became so poor that one day he had to sell his beautiful tail to a hawker, who wanted it for driving away flies.

'Oh, Pinocchio,' sobbed the fox, 'give something to two poor invalids.'

'Invalids,' repeated the cat.

'Good-bye, scoundrels!' answered the puppet. 'You cheated me once, but you never will again.'

'Believe me, Pinocchio, we are really poor and miserable.'

'Poor and miserable!' repeated the cat.

'If you are poor, serve you right. Remember the proverb, "Easy come, easy go!" Good-bye, scoundrels!'

'Have pity on us!'

'On us!'

'Good-bye, scoundrels! Remember the proverb, "The devil's flour is all bran".'

'Do not abandon us!'

'Us!' repeated the cat.

'Good-bye, scoundrels! Remember the proverb, "He who steals his neighbour's cloak, ends his life without a shirt"!'

Speaking thus, Pinocchio and Geppetto went peacefully on their way; but they had hardly gone another hundred steps when they noticed, at the end of a narrow path in a meadow, a charming little cottage made of bricks and tiles, with a roof of straw.

'Someone must live in that cottage,' said Pinocchio. 'Let us knock on the door.'

'Who is it?' said a tiny voice, inside.

'A poor father and his poor son, with no bread, and without a home,' answered the puppet.

'Turn the key, and the door will open,' said the tiny voice.

Pinocchio turned the key, and the door opened. They went in and looked around, but they saw nobody.

'Where can the house-owner be?' asked Pinocchio in amazement.

'Here I am, up here.'

Father and son looked up at the roof, and there on a little crossbeam was the talking cricket.

'Oh, my dear cricket!' said Pinocchio, with a polite bow.

'So I am your "dear cricket" now, am I? Do you remember when you chased me from your home by throwing a hammer at me?'

'You are right, cricket. Drive me away, too. Throw a hammer at me, too! But for pity's sake don't drive away my poor father.'

'I shall have pity on both of you, father and son, but I wanted you to remember the cruel treatment I received. It may teach you that in this world, we should treat everyone kindly as far as it is possible, that we ourselves may be treated kindly when we need it.'

'You are right, cricket. You are absolutely right, and I'll remember the lesson. But tell me, how did you manage to buy this beautiful cottage?'

'This cottage was given to me yesterday, by a kind goat with beautiful blue hair.'

'What has become of the goat?'

'I don't know.'

'When will she be back?'

'She will never be back. She left yesterday, very sad, and bleating as if to say, "Poor Pinocchio, I shall never see him again! The shark must have eaten him by now"!'

'Did she say that? It must have been the fairy – it was surely the fairy – my dear little fairy!' cried Pinocchio, sobbing bitterly, and bursting into floods of tears.

When he had had a good cry, he dried his eyes, and made a good bed of straw for old Geppetto. Then he said to the talking cricket, 'Tell me, cricket, where can I get a cup of milk for my poor father?'

'Giangio, the gardener, lives three paddocks away from here. He has some cows. If you go there, you might get some milk.'

Pinocchio ran at once to Giangio's house, who asked him, 'How much milk do you want?'

'I want a cupful.'

'A cup of milk costs a penny. First give me a penny.'

'I haven't even a farthing,' answered Pinocchio, very sadly.

'That's too bad,' answered the gardener. 'If you haven't even a farthing, why should I have milk for you?'

'Never mind!' said Pinocchio, and he turned to go away.

'Wait a minute,' said Giangio. 'Perhaps we can manage it. Will you turn the windlass for me?'

'What is a windlass?'

'It's a machine that carries up water from the well to water the garden.'

'I'll try.'

'Well, if you will draw a hundred buckets of water, I'll give you a cup of milk.'

'I'll do it.'

Giangio took the puppet into the garden, and showed him how to turn the windlass. Pinocchio started at once, but before he could draw the hundred buckets of water he was perspiring from head to foot. He had never worked like that before.

'It was my donkey's work until today,' said the gardener, 'but the poor beast is dying.'

'May I go and see him?' asked Pinocchio.

'Certainly.'

When Pinocchio came into the stable, he saw a fine donkey on the straw. He was dying of hunger and hard work.

He looked at him, and said to himself, trembling, 'I think I know that donkey. His face isn't new to me.' And, coming near him he said in ass idiom, 'Who are you?'

At this question the dying donkey opened his eyes and answered in the same language, 'I . . . am . . . Lamp . . . wick . . .' After which he closed his eyes and died.

'Oh, poor Lampwick!' murmured Pinocchio and, taking some straw, he wiped the tears that were running down his cheek.

'Are you so sorry for this donkey that doesn't cost you anything?' said the gardener. 'What shall I do, I who paid for it in hard cash?'

'I'll tell you . . . he was my friend.'

'Your friend?'

'Yes, he was a schoolmate of mine.'

'What!' shouted Giangio, bursting out laughing. 'What! You had an ass for a schoolmate? Fine lessons you must have had in your school!'

The puppet was so shamed by these words that he did not answer, but took his milk and returned to the cottage.

From that day, for over five months, he got up before dawn every morning to turn the windlass, so as to earn the cup of milk for his father. But that was not all; in his spare time, he learned how to weave baskets of reeds. He sold them, and they had enough to pay for all their needs. He also made a fine little cart, in which he took his father for a ride and a breath of fresh air when the weather was fine.

When evening came, he practised reading and writing. For a few pennies he bought a large book in the city, whose index and title page were missing; but it served him very well. He cut a pen out of a small twig and, as he had neither ink nor inkwell, he used a little bottle of cherry and blackberry juice.

Because of his ingenuity and his diligence, his father, whose health was still very bad, could live very comfortably. He even saved two shillings, to buy himself a new suit.

One morning he said to his father, 'I'm going to the market today, to buy myself a new jacket, a cap, and a pair of shoes. When I come back,' he added, laughing, 'I shall be so beautiful that you'll mistake me for a great lord.'

He felt very happy and satisfied as he ran along. Suddenly he heard someone speaking to him. He turned and saw a fine snail coming from the hedge.

'Don't you know me?' said the snail.

'Perhaps, but I'm not sure . . .'

'Don't you remember that snail who was the blue-haired fairy's maid? Don't you remember how I came downstairs to let you in, and how I found you with your foot sticking in the door?'

'I remember everything!' cried Pinocchio. 'Tell me quickly, dear snail, where did you leave my good fairy? What is she doing? Has she pardoned me? Does she still remember me? Does she love me still? Is she very far from here? Can I go and see her?'

Pinocchio asked all these questions as fast as he could, without once stopping to breathe.

But the snail answered with her usual slowness, 'My dear Pinocchio, the poor fairy is sick in a hospital!'

'In a hospital?'

'Unhappily, yes. Harassed by a thousand calamities, she is very, very ill, and she hasn't the money to buy even a tiny piece of bread.'

'Is it possible? Oh, how dreadful! Oh, the poor fairy! The poor fairy! If I had a million pounds, I'd give them to her; but I have only two shillings. Take them; I was just going to buy myself a new suit. Take them quickly, snail, to the kind fairy.'

'But your new suit?'

'What does a new suit matter? I'd even sell these rags I have on if I could help her. Go, snail, hurry! If you will come back again in two days, I may be able to give you a little more. I've worked until now for my father; from now on, I'll work five hours longer every day, for my kind mother. Good-bye, snail, I'll expect you in two days.'

The snail, most surprisingly, began to run like a lizard in summer.

When Pinocchio arrived back, his father asked him, 'Where is your new suit?'

'I couldn't find one that fitted me. Never mind! I'll buy it next time.'

That evening, instead of working until ten o'clock, Pinocchio worked until midnight; and instead of making eight baskets, he made sixteen.

Then he went to bed, and fell asleep. As he slept, he dreamed he saw the fairy, lovely and smiling, who gave him a kiss, saying, 'Brave Pinocchio! In return for your good heart I forgive you all your past misdeeds. Children who love their parents, and help them when they are sick and poor, are worthy of praise and love, even if they are not models of obedience and good behaviour. Be good in future, and you will be happy.'

Then the dream ended, and Pinocchio awoke, full of amazement.

You can imagine how astonished he was when he saw that he was no longer a puppet, but a real boy just like other boys. He looked round; but instead of the straw walls of the cottage, he saw a lovely little room simply though beautifully furnished and papered. He jumped out of bed, and found a pretty new suit, a new cap, and a pair of boots as pretty as a picture.

When he was dressed, he put his hands in his pockets,

and found there a little ivory purse on which these words were written: '*The blue-haired fairy returns Pinocchio's two shillings, and thanks him for his good heart.*'

He opened the purse, and, instead of two silver shillings, there were twenty gold pieces in it.

Then he went to look in the mirror, but he could not recognize himself. Instead of the usual picture of a wooden puppet, he saw the expressive, intelligent face of a good-looking boy, with brown hair and blue eyes, who looked contented and full of joy.

Amidst all these wonders, Pinocchio no longer knew whether he was awake or asleep with his eyes open.

'And my father, where is he?' he cried, suddenly. He hurried into the next room and there he saw old Geppetto, well, and brisk, and good-natured, as he had been before. He had again taken up his old art of wood-carving, and just then he was planning a beautiful cornice, decorated with leaves and flowers, and animal heads.

'Daddy, tell me, what is the meaning of this sudden change?' asked Pinocchio, hugging and kissing him.

'This sudden change is all due to you,' answered Geppetto.

'Why is it due to me?'

'Because when children who were naughty become good, it gives a new smiling appearance to the whole family.'

'And the old wooden Pinocchio, where is he?'

'There he is,' answered Geppetto, pointing to a large puppet that was leaning against a chair with his head on on side, his arms hanging loosely, and his legs bent and crossed, so that it was a miracle that he could stand there.

Pinocchio turned and looked at him for a moment, and then said to himself, contentedly,

'How ridiculous I was when I was a puppet! And how happy I am to have become a real boy!'

CLASSIC LITERATURE: WORDS AND PHRASES
adapted from the *Collins English Dictionary*

Accoucheur NOUN a male midwife or doctor ❑ *I think my sister must have had some general idea that I was a young offender whom an Accoucheur Policeman had taken up (on my birthday) and delivered over to her* (*Great Expectations* by Charles Dickens)

addled ADJ confused and unable to think properly ❑ *But she counted and counted till she got that addled* (*The Adventures of Huckleberry Finn* by Mark Twain)

admiration NOUN amazement or wonder ❑ *lifting up his hands and eyes by way of admiration* (*Gulliver's Travels* by Jonathan Swift)

afeard ADJ afeard means afraid ❑ *shake it–and don't be afeard* (*The Adventures of Huckleberry Finn* by Mark Twain)

affected VERB affected means followed ❑ *Hadst thou affected sweet divinity* (*Doctor Faustus 5.2* by Christopher Marlowe)

aground ADV when a boat runs aground, it touches the ground in a shallow part of the water and gets stuck ❑ *what kep' you?–boat get aground?* (*The Adventures of Huckleberry Finn* by Mark Twain)

ague NOUN a fever in which the patient has alternate hot and cold shivering fits ❑ *his exposure to the wet and cold had brought on fever and ague* (*Oliver Twist* by Charles Dickens)

alchemy ADJ false or worthless ❑ *all wealth alchemy* (*The Sun Rising* by John Donne)

all alike PHRASE the same all the time ❑ *Love, all alike* (*The Sun Rising* by John Donne)

alow and aloft PHRASE alow means in the lower part or bottom, and aloft means on the top, so alow and aloft means on the top and in the bottom or throughout ❑ *Someone's turned the chest out alow and aloft* (*Treasure Island* by Robert Louis Stevenson)

ambuscade NOUN ambuscade is not a proper word. Tom means an ambush, which is when a group of people attack their enemies, after hiding and waiting for them ❑ *and so we would lie in ambuscade, as he called it* (*The Adventures of Huckleberry Finn* by Mark Twain)

amiable ADJ likeable or pleasant ❑ *Such amiable qualities must speak for themselves* (*Pride and Prejudice* by Jane Austen)

amulet NOUN an amulet is a charm thought to drive away evil spirits. ❑ *uttered phrases at once occult and familiar, like the amulet worn on the heart* (*Silas Marner* by George Eliot)

amusement NOUN here amusement means a strange and disturbing puzzle ❑ *this was an amusement the other way* (*Robinson Crusoe* by Daniel Defoe)

ancient NOUN an ancient was the flag displayed on a ship to show which country it belongs to. It is also called the ensign ❑ *her ancient and pendants out* (*Robinson Crusoe* by Daniel Defoe)

antic ADJ here antic means horrible or grotesque ❑ *armed and dressed after a very antic manner* (*Gulliver's Travels* by Jonathan Swift)

antics NOUN antics is an old word meaning clowns, or people who do silly things to make other people laugh ❑ *And point like antics at his triple crown* (*Doctor Faustus 3.2* by Christopher Marlowe)

appanage NOUN an appanage is a living allowance ❑ *As if loveliness were* *not the special prerogative of woman–her legitimate appanage and heritage! (Jane Eyre* by Charlotte Brontë)

appended VERB appended means attached or added to ❑ *and these words appended (Treasure Island* by Robert Louis Stevenson)

approver NOUN an approver is someone who gives evidence against someone he used to work with ❑ *Mr. Noah Claypole: receiving a free pardon from the Crown in consequence of being admitted approver against Fagin (Oliver Twist* by Charles Dickens)

areas NOUN the areas is the space, below street level, in front of the basement of a house ❑ *The Dodger had a vicious propensity, too, of pulling the caps from the heads of small boys and tossing them down areas (Oliver Twist* by Charles Dickens)

argument NOUN theme or important idea or subject which runs through a piece of writing ❑ *Thrice needful to the argument which now (The Prelude* by William Wordsworth)

artificially ADJ artfully or cleverly ❑ *and he with a sharp flint sharpened very artificially (Gulliver's Travels* by Jonathan Swift)

artist NOUN here artist means a skilled workman ❑ *This man was a most ingenious artist (Gulliver's Travels* by Jonathan Swift)

assizes NOUN assizes were regular court sessions which a visiting judge was in charge of ❑ *you shall hang at the next assizes (Treasure Island* by Robert Louis Stevenson)

attraction NOUN gravitation, or Newton's theory of gravitation ❑ *he predicted the same fate to attraction (Gulliver's Travels* by Jonathan Swift)

aver VERB to aver is to claim something strongly ❑ *for Jem Rodney, the mole catcher, averred that one evening as*

he was returning homeward (Silas Marner by George Eliot)

baby NOUN here baby means doll, which is a child's toy that looks like a small person ❑ *and skilful dressing her baby (Gulliver's Travels* by Jonathan Swift)

bagatelle NOUN bagatelle is a game rather like billiards and pool ❑ *Breakfast had been ordered at a pleasant little tavern, a mile or so away upon the rising ground beyond the green; and there was a bagatelle board in the room, in case we should desire to unbend our minds after the solemnity. (Great Expectations* by Charles Dickens)

bah EXCLAM Bah is an exclamation of frustration or anger ❑ *"Bah," said Scrooge. (A Christmas Carol* by Charles Dickens)

bairn NOUN a northern word for child ❑ *Who has taught you those fine words, my bairn? (Wuthering Heights* by Emily Brontë)

bait VERB to bait means to stop on a journey to take refreshment ❑ *So, when they stopped to bait the horse, and ate and drank and enjoyed themselves, I could touch nothing that they touched, but kept my fast unbroken. (David Copperfield* by Charles Dickens)

balustrade NOUN a balustrade is a row of vertical columns that form railings ❑ *but I mean to say you might have got a hearse up that staircase, and taken it broadwise, with the splinter-bar towards the wall, and the door towards the balustrades: and done it easy (A Christmas Carol* by Charles Dickens)

bandbox NOUN a large lightweight box for carrying bonnets or hats ❑ *I am glad I bought my bonnet, if it is only for the fun of having another bandbox (Pride and Prejudice* by Jane Austen)

barren NOUN a barren here is a stretch or expanse of barren land ❑ *a line of upright stones, continued the* *length of the barren* (*Wuthering Heights* by Emily Brontë)

basin NOUN a basin was a cup without a handle ❑ *who is drinking his tea out of a basin* (*Wuthering Heights* by Emily Brontë)

battalia NOUN the order of battle ❑ *till I saw part of his army in battalia* (*Gulliver's Travels* by Jonathan Swift)

battery NOUN a Battery is a fort or a place where guns are positioned ❑ *You bring the lot to me, at that old Battery over yonder* (*Great Expectations* by Charles Dickens)

battledore and shuttlecock NOUN The game battledore and shuttlecock was an early version of the game now known as badminton. The aim of the early game was simply to keep the shuttlecock from hitting the ground. ❑ *Battledore and shuttlecock's a wery good game vhen you an't the shuttlecock and two lawyers the battledores, in which case it gets too excitin' to be pleasant* (*Pickwick Papers* by Charles Dickens)

beadle NOUN a beadle was a local official who had power over the poor ❑ *But these impertinences were speedily checked by the evidence of the surgeon, and the testimony of the beadle* (*Oliver Twist* by Charles Dickens)

bearings NOUN the bearings of a place are the measurements or directions that are used to find or locate it ❑ *the bearings of the island* (*Treasure Island* by Robert Louis Stevenson)

beaufet NOUN a beaufet was a sideboard ❑ *and sweet-cake from the beaufet* (*Emma* by Jane Austen)

beck NOUN a beck is a small stream ❑ *a beck which follows the bend of the glen* (*Wuthering Heights* by Emily Brontë)

bedight VERB decorated ❑ *and bedight with Christmas holly stuck into the top.* (*A Christmas Carol* by Charles Dickens)

Bedlam NOUN Bedlam was a lunatic asylum in London which had statues carved by Caius Gabriel Cibber at its entrance ❑ *Bedlam, and those carved maniacs at the gates* (*The Prelude* by William Wordsworth)

beeves NOUN oxen or castrated bulls which are animals used for pulling vehicles or carrying things ❑ *to deliver in every morning six beeves* (*Gulliver's Travels* by Jonathan Swift)

begot VERB created or caused ❑ *Begot in thee* (*On His Mistress* by John Donne)

behoof NOUN behoof means benefit ❑ *"Yes, young man," said he, releasing the handle of the article in question, retiring a step or two from my table, and speaking for the behoof of the landlord and waiter at the door* (*Great Expectations* by Charles Dickens)

berth NOUN a berth is a bed on a boat ❑ *this is the berth for me* (*Treasure Island* by Robert Louis Stevenson)

bevers NOUN a bever was a snack, or small portion of food, eaten between main meals ❑ *that buys me thirty meals a day and ten bevers* (*Doctor Faustus 2.1* by Christopher Marlowe)

bilge water NOUN the bilge is the widest part of a ship's bottom, and the bilge water is the dirty water that collects there ❑ *no gush of bilge-water had turned it to fetid puddle* (*Jane Eyre* by Charlotte Brontë)

bills NOUN bills is an old term meaning prescription. A prescription is the piece of paper on which your doctor writes an order for medicine and which you give to a chemist to get the medicine ❑ *Are not thy bills hung up as monuments* (*Doctor Faustus 1.1* by Christopher Marlowe)

black cap NOUN a judge wore a black cap when he was about to sentence a prisoner to death ❑ *The judge assumed the black cap, and the* *prisoner still stood with the same air and gesture.* (*Oliver Twist* by Charles Dickens)

black gentleman NOUN this was another word for the devil ❑ *for she is as impatient as the black gentleman* (*Emma* by Jane Austen)

boot-jack NOUN a wooden device to help take boots off ❑ *The speaker appeared to throw a boot-jack, or some such article, at the person he addressed* (*Oliver Twist* by Charles Dickens)

booty NOUN booty means treasure or prizes ❑ *would be inclined to give up their booty in payment of the dead man's debts* (*Treasure Island* by Robert Louis Stevenson)

Bow Street runner PHRASE Bow Street runners were the first British police force, set up by the author Henry Fielding in the eighteenth century ❑ *as would have convinced a judge or a Bow Street runner* (*Treasure Island* by Robert Louis Stevenson)

brawn NOUN brawn is a dish of meat which is set in jelly ❑ *Heaped up upon the floor, to form a kind of throne, were turkeys, geese, game, poultry, brawn, great joints of meat, sucking-pigs* (*A Christmas Carol* by Charles Dickens)

bray VERB when a donkey brays, it makes a loud, harsh sound ❑ *and she doesn't bray like a jackass* (*The Adventures of Huckleberry Finn* by Mark Twain)

break VERB in order to train a horse you first have to break it ❑ *"If a high-mettled creature like this," said he, "can't be broken by fair means, she will never be good for anything"* (*Black Beauty* by Anna Sewell)

bullyragging VERB bullyragging is an old word which means bullying. To bullyrag someone is to threaten or force someone to do something they don't want to do ❑ *and a lot of loafers bullyragging him for sport* (*The Adventures of Huckleberry Finn* by Mark Twain)

but PREP except for (this) ❑ *but this, all pleasures fancies be* (*The Good-Morrow* by John Donne)

by hand PHRASE by hand was a common expression of the time meaning that baby had been fed either using a spoon or a bottle rather than by breast-feeding ❑ *My sister, Mrs. Joe Gargery, was more than twenty years older than I, and had established a great reputation with herself . . . because she had bought me up 'by hand'* (*Great Expectations* by Charles Dickens)

bye-spots NOUN bye-spots are lonely places ❑ *and bye-spots of tales rich with indigenous produce* (*The Prelude* by William Wordsworth)

calico NOUN calico is plain white fabric made from cotton ❑ *There was two old dirty calico dresses* (*The Adventures of Huckleberry Finn* by Mark Twain)

camp-fever NOUN camp-fever was another word for the disease typhus ❑ *during a severe camp-fever* (*Emma* by Jane Austen)

cant NOUN cant is insincere or empty talk ❑ *"Man," said the Ghost, "if man you be in heart, not adamant, forbear that wicked cant until you have discovered What the surplus is, and Where it is."* (*A Christmas Carol* by Charles Dickens)

canty ADJ canty means lively, full of life ❑ *My mother lived til eighty, a canty dame to the last* (*Wuthering Heights* by Emily Brontë)

canvas VERB to canvas is to discuss ❑ *We think so very differently on this point Mr Knightley, that there can be no use in canvassing it* (*Emma* by Jane Austen)

capital ADJ capital means excellent or extremely good ❑ *for it's capital, so shady, light, and big* (*Little Women* by Louisa May Alcott)

capstan NOUN a capstan is a device used on a ship to lift sails and anchors ❑ *capstans going, ships going out to sea, and unintelligible* *sea creatures roaring curses over the bulwarks at respondent lightermen* (*Great Expectations* by Charles Dickens)

case-bottle NOUN a square bottle designed to fit with others into a case ❏ *The spirit being set before him in a huge case-bottle, which had originally come out of some ship's locker* (*The Old Curiosity Shop* by Charles Dickens)

casement NOUN casement is a word meaning window. The teacher in Nicholas Nickleby misspells window showing what a bad teacher he is ❏ *W-i-n, win, d-e-r, der, winder, a casement.'* (*Nicholas Nickleby* by Charles Dickens)

cataleptic ADJ a cataleptic fit is one in which the victim goes into a trance-like state and remains still for a long time ❏ *It was at this point in their history that Silas's cataleptic fit occurred during the prayer-meeting* (*Silas Marner* by George Eliot)

cauldron NOUN a cauldron is a large cooking pot made of metal ❏ *stirring a large cauldron which seemed to be full of soup* (*Alice's Adventures in Wonderland* by Lewis Carroll)

cephalic ADJ cephalic means to do with the head ❏ *with ink composed of a cephalic tincture* (*Gulliver's Travels* by Jonathan Swift)

chaise and four NOUN a closed four-wheel carriage pulled by four horses ❏ *he came down on Monday in a chaise and four to see the place* (*Pride and Prejudice* by Jane Austen)

chamberlain NOUN the main servant in a household ❏ *In those times a bed was always to be got there at any hour of the night, and the chamberlain, letting me in at his ready wicket, lighted the candle next in order on his shelf* (*Great Expectations* by Charles Dickens)

characters NOUN distinguishing marks ❏ *Impressed upon all forms the characters* (*The Prelude* by William Wordsworth)

chary ADJ cautious ❏ *I should have been chary of discussing my guardian too freely even with her* (*Great Expectations* by Charles Dickens)

cherishes VERB here cherishes means cheers or brightens ❏ *some philosophic song of Truth that cherishes our daily life* (*The Prelude* by William Wordsworth)

chickens' meat PHRASE chickens' meat is an old term which means chickens' feed or food ❏ *I had shook a bag of chickens' meat out in that place* (*Robinson Crusoe* by Daniel Defoe)

chimeras NOUN a chimera is an unrealistic idea or a wish which is unlikely to be fulfilled ❏ *with many other wild impossible chimeras* (*Gulliver's Travels* by Jonathan Swift)

chines NOUN chine is a cut of meat that includes part or all of the backbone of the animal ❏ *and they found hams and chines uncut* (*Silas Marner* by George Eliot)

chits NOUN chits is a slang word which means girls ❏ *I hate affected, niminy-piminy chits!* (*Little Women* by Louisa May Alcott)

chopped VERB chopped means come suddenly or accidentally ❏ *if I had chopped upon them* (*Robinson Crusoe* by Daniel Defoe)

chute NOUN a narrow channel ❏ *One morning about day-break, I found a canoe and crossed over a chute to the main shore* (*The Adventures of Huckleberry Finn* by Mark Twain)

circumspection NOUN careful observation of events and circumstances; caution ❏ *I honour your circumspection* (*Pride and Prejudice* by Jane Austen)

clambered VERB clambered means to climb somewhere with difficulty, usually using your hands and your feet ❏ *he clambered up and down stairs* (*Treasure Island* by Robert Louis Stevenson)

clime NOUN climate ❑ *no season knows nor clime* (*The Sun Rising* by John Donne)

clinched VERB clenched ❑ *the tops whereof I could but just reach with my fist clinched* (*Gulliver's Travels* by Jonathan Swift)

close chair NOUN a close chair is a sedan chair, which is an covered chair which has room for one person. The sedan chair is carried on two poles by two men, one in front and one behind ❑ *persuaded even the Empress herself to let me hold her in her close chair* (*Gulliver's Travels* by Jonathan Swift)

clown NOUN clown here means peasant or person who lives off the land ❑ *In ancient days by emperor and clown* (*Ode on a Nightingale* by John Keats)

coalheaver NOUN a coalheaver loaded coal onto ships using a spade ❑ *Good, strong, wholesome medicine, as was given with great success to two Irish labourers and a coalheaver* (*Oliver Twist* by Charles Dickens)

coal-whippers NOUN men who worked at docks using machines to load coal onto ships ❑ *here, were colliers by the score and score, with the coal-whippers plunging off stages on deck* (*Great Expectations* by Charles Dickens)

cobweb NOUN a cobweb is the net which a spider makes for catching insects ❑ *the walls and ceilings were all hung round with cobwebs* (*Gulliver's Travels* by Jonathan Swift)

coddling VERB coddling means to treat someone too kindly or protect them too much ❑ *and I've been coddling the fellow as if I'd been his grandmother* (*Little Women* by Louisa May Alcott)

coil NOUN coil means noise or fuss or disturbance ❑ *What a coil is there?* (*Doctor Faustus 4.7* by Christopher Marlowe)

collared VERB to collar something is a slang term which means to capture.

In this sentence, it means he stole it [the money] ❑ *he collared it* (*The Adventures of Huckleberry Finn* by Mark Twain)

colling VERB colling is an old word which means to embrace and kiss ❑ *and no clasping and colling at all* (*Tess of the D'Urbervilles* by Thomas Hardy)

colloquies NOUN colloquy is a formal conversation or dialogue ❑ *Such colloquies have occupied many a pair of pale-faced weavers* (*Silas Marner* by George Eliot)

comfit NOUN sugar-covered pieces of fruit or nut eaten as sweets ❑ *and pulled out a box of comfits* (*Alice's Adventures in Wonderland* by Lewis Carroll)

coming out VERB when a girl came out in society it meant she was of marriageable age. In order to 'come out' girls were expecting to attend balls and other parties during a season ❑ *The younger girls formed hopes of coming out a year or two sooner than they might otherwise have done* (*Pride and Prejudice* by Jane Austen)

commit VERB commit means arrest or stop ❑ *Commit the rascals* (*Doctor Faustus 4.7* by Christopher Marlowe)

commodious ADJ commodious means convenient ❑ *the most commodious and effectual ways* (*Gulliver's Travels* by Jonathan Swift)

commons NOUN commons is an old term meaning food shared with others ❑ *his pauper assistants ranged themselves behind him; the gruel was served out; and a long grace was said over the short commons.* (*Oliver Twist* by Charles Dickens)

complacency NOUN here complacency means a desire to please others. To-day complacency means feeling pleased with oneself without good reason. ❑ *'Twas thy power that raised the first complacency in me* (*The Prelude* by William Wordsworth)

complaisance NOUN complaisance was eagerness to please ❏ *we cannot wonder at his complaisance* (*Pride and Prejudice* by Jane Austen)

complaisant ADJ complaisant means polite ❏ *extremely cheerful and complaisant to their guest* (*Gulliver's Travels* by Jonathan Swift)

conning VERB conning means learning by heart ❏ *Or conning more* (*The Prelude* by William Wordsworth)

consequent NOUN consequence ❏ *as avarice is the necessary consequent of old age* (*Gulliver's Travels* by Jonathan Swift)

consorts NOUN concerts ❏ *The King, who delighted in music, had frequent consorts at Court* (*Gulliver's Travels* by Jonathan Swift)

conversible ADJ conversible meant easy to talk to, companionable ❏ *He can be a conversible companion* (*Pride and Prejudice* by Jane Austen)

copper NOUN a copper is a large pot that can be heated directly over a fire ❏ *He gazed in stupefied astonishment on the small rebel for some seconds, and then clung for support to the copper* (*Oliver Twist* by Charles Dickens)

copper-stick NOUN a copper-stick is the long piece of wood used to stir washing in the copper (or boiler) which was usually the biggest cooking pot in the house ❏ *It was Christmas Eve, and I had to stir the pudding for next day, with a copper-stick, from seven to eight by the Dutch clock* (*Great Expectations* by Charles Dickens)

counting-house NOUN a counting house is a place where accountants work ❏ *Once upon a time–of all the good days in the year, on Christmas Eve–old Scrooge sat busy in his countinghouse* (*A Christmas Carol* by Charles Dickens)

courtier NOUN a courtier is someone who attends the king or queen–a member of the court ❏ *next the ten courtiers;* (*Alice's Adventures in Wonderland* by Lewis Carroll)

covies NOUN covies were flocks of partridges ❏ *and will save all of the best covies for you* (*Pride and Prejudice* by Jane Austen)

cowed VERB cowed means frightened or intimidated ❏ *it cowed me more than the pain* (*Treasure Island* by Robert Louis Stevenson)

cozened VERB cozened means tricked or deceived ❏ *Do you remember, sir, how you cozened me* (*Doctor Faustus 4.7* by Christopher Marlowe)

cravats NOUN a cravat is a folded cloth that a man wears wrapped around his neck as a decorative item of clothing ❏ *we'd'a' slept in our cravats to-night* (*The Adventures of Huckleberry Finn* by Mark Twain)

crock and dirt PHRASE crock and dirt is an old expression meaning soot and dirt ❏ *and the mare catching cold at the door, and the boy grimed with crock and dirt* (*Great Expectations* by Charles Dickens)

crockery NOUN here crockery means pottery ❏ *By one of the parrots was a cat made of crockery* (*The Adventures of Huckleberry Finn* by Mark Twain)

crooked sixpence PHRASE it was considered unlucky to have a bent sixpence ❏ *You've got the beauty, you see, and I've got the luck, so you must keep me by you for your crooked sixpence* (*Silas Marner* by George Eliot)

croquet NOUN croquet is a traditional English summer game in which players try to hit wooden balls through hoops ❏ *and once she remembered trying to box her own ears for having cheated herself in a game of croquet* (*Alice's Adventures in Wonderland* by Lewis Carroll)

cross PREP across ❏ *The two great streets, which run cross and divide it into four quarters* (*Gulliver's Travels* by Jonathan Swift)

culpable ADJ if you are culpable for something it means you are to blame ❏ *deep are the sorrows that spring from false ideas for which no man is culpable.* (*Silas Marner* by George Eliot)

cultured ADJ cultivated ❏ *Nor less when spring had warmed the cultured Vale* (*The Prelude* by William Wordsworth)

cupidity NOUN cupidity is greed ❏ *These people hated me with the hatred of cupidity and disappointment.* (*Great Expectations* by Charles Dickens)

curricle NOUN an open two-wheeled carriage with one seat for the driver and space for a single passenger ❏ *and they saw a lady and a gentleman in a curricle* (*Pride and Prejudice* by Jane Austen)

cynosure NOUN a cynosure is something that strongly attracts attention or admiration ❏ *Then I thought of Eliza and Georgiana; I beheld one the cynosure of a ballroom, the other the inmate of a convent cell* (*Jane Eyre* by Charlotte Brontë)

dalliance NOUN someone's dalliance with something is a brief involvement with it ❏ *nor sporting in the dalliance of love* (*Doctor Faustus Chorus* by Christopher Marlowe)

darkling ADV darkling is an archaic way of saying in the dark ❏ *Darkling I listen* (*Ode on a Nightingale* by John Keats)

delf-case NOUN a sideboard for holding dishes and crockery ❏ *at the pewter dishes and delf-case* (*Wuthering Heights* by Emily Brontë)

determined ■ VERB here determined means ended ❏ *and be out of vogue when that was determined* (*Gulliver's Travels* by Jonathan Swift) ■ VERB determined can mean to have been learned or found especially by investigation or experience ❏ *All the sensitive feelings it wounded so cruelly, all the shame and misery it kept alive within my breast, became more poignant as I*

thought of this; and I determined that the life was unendurable (*David Copperfield* by Charles Dickens)

Deuce NOUN a slang term for the Devil ❏ *Ah, I dare say I did. Deuce take me, he added suddenly, I know I did. I find I am not quite unscrewed yet.* (*Great Expectations* by Charles Dickens)

diabolical ADJ diabolical means devilish or evil ❏ *and with a thousand diabolical expressions* (*Treasure Island* by Robert Louis Stevenson)

direction NOUN here direction means address ❏ *Elizabeth was not surprised at it, as Jane had written the direction remarkably ill* (*Pride and Prejudice* by Jane Austen)

discover VERB to make known or announce ❏ *the Emperor would discover the secret while I was out of his power* (*Gulliver's Travels* by Jonathan Swift)

dissemble VERB hide or conceal ❏ *Dissemble nothing* (*On His Mistress* by John Donne)

dissolve VERB dissolve here means to release from life, to die ❏ *Fade far away, dissolve, and quite forget* (*Ode on a Nightingale* by John Keats)

distrain VERB to distrain is to seize the property of someone who is in debt in compensation for the money owed ❏ *for he's threatening to distrain for it* (*Silas Marner* by George Eliot)

Divan NOUN a Divan was originally a Turkish council of state–the name was transferred to the couches they sat on and is used to mean this in English ❏ *Mr Brass applauded this picture very much, and the bed being soft and comfortable, Mr Quilp determined to use it, both as a sleeping place by night and as a kind of Divan by day.* (*The Old Curiosity Shop* by Charles Dickens)

divorcement NOUN separation ❏ *By all pains which want and divorcement* *hath* (*On His Mistress* by John Donne)

dog in the manger, PHRASE this phrase describes someone who prevents you from enjoying something that they themselves have no need for ❑ *You are a dog in the manger, Cathy, and desire no one to be loved but yourself* (*Wuthering Heights* by Emily Brontë)

dolorifuge NOUN dolorifuge is a word which Thomas Hardy invented. It means pain-killer or comfort ❑ *as a species of dolorifuge* (*Tess of the D'Urbervilles* by Thomas Hardy)

dome NOUN building ❑ *that river and that mouldering dome* (*The Prelude* by William Wordsworth)

domestic PHRASE here domestic means a person's management of the house ❑ *to give some account of my domestic* (*Gulliver's Travels* by Jonathan Swift)

dunce NOUN a dunce is another word for idiot ❑ *Do you take me for a dunce? Go on?* (*Alice's Adventures in Wonderland* by Lewis Carroll)

Ecod EXCLAM a slang exclamation meaning 'oh God!' ❑ *"Ecod," replied Wemmick, shaking his head, "that's not my trade."* (*Great Expectations* by Charles Dickens)

egg-hot NOUN an egg-hot (see also 'flip' and 'negus') was a hot drink made from beer and eggs, sweetened with nutmeg ❑ *She fainted when she saw me return, and made a little jug of egg-hot afterwards to console us while we talked it over.* (*David Copperfield* by Charles Dickens)

encores NOUN an encore is a short extra performance at the end of a longer one, which the entertainer gives because the audience has enthusiastically asked for it ❑ *we want a little something to answer encores with, anyway* (*The Adventures of Huckleberry Finn* by Mark Twain)

equipage NOUN an elegant and impressive carriage ❑ *and besides, the equipage did not answer to any of*

their neighbours (*Pride and Prejudice* by Jane Austen)

exordium NOUN an exordium is the opening part of a speech ❑ *"Now, Handel," as if it were the grave beginning of a portentous business exordium, he had suddenly given up that tone* (*Great Expectations* by Charles Dickens)

expect VERB here expect means to wait for ❑ *to expect his farther commands* (*Gulliver's Travels* by Jonathan Swift)

familiars NOUN familiars means spirits or devils who come to someone when they are called ❑ *I'll turn all the lice about thee into familiars* (*Doctor Faustus 1.4* by Christopher Marlowe)

fantods NOUN a fantod is a person who fidgets or can't stop moving nervously ❑ *It most give me the fantods* (*The Adventures of Huckleberry Finn* by Mark Twain)

farthing NOUN a farthing is an old unit of British currency which was worth a quarter of a penny ❑ *Not a farthing less. A great many back-payments are included in it, I assure you.* (*A Christmas Carol* by Charles Dickens)

farthingale NOUN a hoop worn under a skirt to extend it ❑ *A bell with an old voice–which I dare say in its time had often said to the house, Here is the green farthingale* (*Great Expectations* by Charles Dickens)

favours NOUN here favours is an old word which means ribbons ❑ *A group of humble mourners entered the gate: wearing white favours* (*Oliver Twist* by Charles Dickens)

feigned VERB pretend or pretending ❑ *not my feigned page* (*On His Mistress* by John Donne)

fence ■ NOUN a fence is someone who receives and sells stolen goods ❑ *What are you up to? Ill-treating the boys, you covetous, avaricious, in-sa-ti-a-ble old fence?* (*Oliver Twist* by

Charles Dickens) ■ NOUN defence or protection ❑ *but honesty hath no fence against superior cunning* (*Gulliver's Travels* by Jonathan Swift)

fess ADJ fess is an old word which means pleased or proud ❑ *You'll be fess enough, my poppet* (*Tess of the D'Urbervilles* by Thomas Hardy)

fettered ADJ fettered means bound in chains or chained ❑ *"You are fettered," said Scrooge, trembling. "Tell me why?"* (*A Christmas Carol* by Charles Dickens)

fidges VERB fidges means fidgets, which is to keep moving your hands slightly because you are nervous or excited ❑ *Look, Jim, how my fingers fidges* (*Treasure Island* by Robert Louis Stevenson)

finger-post NOUN a finger-post is a sign-post showing the direction to different places ❑ *"The gallows,"* continued Fagin, *"the gallows, my dear, is an ugly finger-post, which points out a very short and sharp turning that has stopped many a bold fellow's career on the broad highway."* (*Oliver Twist* by Charles Dickens)

fire-irons NOUN fire-irons are tools kept by the side of the fire to either cook with or look after the fire ❑ *the fire-irons came first* (*Alice's Adventures in Wonderland* by Lewis Carroll)

fire-plug NOUN a fire-plug is another word for a fire hydrant ❑ *The pony looked with great attention into a fire-plug, which was near him, and appeared to be quite absorbed in contemplating it* (*The Old Curiosity Shop* by Charles Dickens)

flank NOUN flank is the side of an animal ❑ *And all her silken flanks with garlands dressed* (*Ode on a Grecian Urn* by John Keats)

flip NOUN a flip is a drink made from warmed ale, sugar, spice and beaten egg ❑ *The events of the day, in combination with the twins, if not with the flip, had made Mrs.*

Micawber hysterical, and she shed tears as she replied (*David Copperfield* by Charles Dickens)

flit VERB flit means to move quickly ❑ *and if he had meant to flit to Thrushcross Grange* (*Wuthering Heights* by Emily Brontë)

floorcloth NOUN a floorcloth was a hard-wearing piece of canvas used instead of carpet ❑ *This avenging phantom was ordered to be on duty at eight on Tuesday morning in the hall (it was two feet square, as charged for floorcloth)* (*Great Expectations* by Charles Dickens)

fly-driver NOUN a fly-driver is a carriage drawn by a single horse ❑ *The fly-drivers, among whom I inquired next, were equally jocose and equally disrespectful* (*David Copperfield* by Charles Dickens)

fob NOUN a small pocket in which a watch is kept ❑ *"Certain," replied the man, drawing a gold watch from his fob* (*Oliver Twist* by Charles Dickens)

folly NOUN folly means foolishness or stupidity ❑ *the folly of beginning a work* (*Robinson Crusoe* by Daniel Defoe)

fond ADJ fond means foolish ❑ *Fond worldling* (*Doctor Faustus 5.2* by Christopher Marlowe)

fondness NOUN silly or foolish affection ❑ *They have no fondness for their colts or foals* (*Gulliver's Travels* by Jonathan Swift)

for his fancy PHRASE for his fancy means for his liking or as he wanted ❑ *and as I did not obey quick enough for his fancy* (*Treasure Island* by Robert Louis Stevenson)

forlorn ADJ lost or very upset ❑ *you are from that day forlorn* (*Gulliver's Travels* by Jonathan Swift)

foster-sister NOUN a foster-sister was someone brought up by the same nurse or in the same household ❑ *I had been his foster-sister* (*Wuthering Heights* by Emily Brontë)

fox-fire NOUN fox-fire is a weak glow that is given off by decaying, rotten wood ❑ *what we must have was a lot of them rotten chunks that's called fox-fire* (*The Adventures of Huckleberry Finn* by Mark Twain)

frozen sea PHRASE the Arctic Ocean ❑ *into the frozen sea* (*Gulliver's Travels* by Jonathan Swift)

gainsay VERB to gainsay something is to say it isn't true or to deny it ❑ *"So she had," cried Scrooge. "You're right. I'll not gainsay it, Spirit. God forbid!"* (*A Christmas Carol* by Charles Dickens)

gaiters NOUN gaiters were leggings made of a cloth or piece of leather which covered the leg from the knee to the ankle ❑ *Mr Knightley was hard at work upon the lower buttons of his thick leather gaiters* (*Emma* by Jane Austen)

galluses NOUN galluses is an old spelling of gallows, and here means suspenders. Suspenders are straps worn over someone's shoulders and fastened to their trousers to prevent the trousers falling down ❑ *and home-knit galluses* (*The Adventures of Huckleberry Finn* by Mark Twain)

galoot NOUN a sailor but also a clumsy person ❑ *and maybe a galoot on it chopping* (*The Adventures of Huckleberry Finn* by Mark Twain)

gayest ADJ gayest means the most lively and bright or merry ❑ *Beth played her gayest march* (*Little Women* by Louisa May Alcott)

gem NOUN here gem means jewellery ❑ *the mountain shook off turf and flower, had only heath for raiment and crag for gem* (*Jane Eyre* by Charlotte Brontë)

giddy ADJ giddy means dizzy ❑ *and I wish you wouldn't keep appearing and vanishing so suddenly; you make one quite giddy.* (*Alice's Adventures in Wonderland* by Lewis Carroll)

gig NOUN a light two-wheeled carriage ❑ *when a gig drove up to the garden gate: out of which there jumped a fat gentleman* (*Oliver Twist* by Charles Dickens)

gladsome ADJ gladsome is an old word meaning glad or happy ❑ *Nobody ever stopped him in the street to say, with gladsome looks* (*A Christmas Carol* by Charles Dickens)

glen NOUN a glen is a small valley; the word is used commonly in Scotland ❑ *a beck which follows the bend of the glen* (*Wuthering Heights* by Emily Brontë)

gravelled VERB gravelled is an old term which means to baffle or defeat someone ❑ *Gravelled the pastors of the German Church* (*Doctor Faustus 1.1* by Christopher Marlowe)

grinder NOUN a grinder was a private tutor ❑ *but that when he had had the happiness of marrying Mrs Pocket very early in his life, he had impaired his prospects and taken up the calling of a Grinder* (*Great Expectations* by Charles Dickens)

gruel NOUN gruel is a thin, watery cornmeal or oatmeal soup ❑ *and the little saucepan of gruel (Scrooge had a cold in his head) upon the hob.* (*A Christmas Carol* by Charles Dickens)

guinea, half a NOUN a half guinea was ten shillings and sixpence ❑ *but lay out half a guinea at Ford's* (*Emma* by Jane Austen)

gull VERB gull is an old term which means to fool or deceive someone ❑ *Hush, I'll gull him supernaturally* (*Doctor Faustus 3.4* by Christopher Marlowe)

gunnel NOUN the gunnel, or gunwhale, is the upper edge of a boat's side ❑ *But he put his foot on the gunnel and rocked her* (*The Adventures of Huckleberry Finn* by Mark Twain)

gunwale NOUN the side of a ship ❑ *He dipped his hand in the water over the boat's gunwale* (*Great Expectations* by Charles Dickens)

Gytrash NOUN a Gytrash is an omen of misfortune to the superstitious, usually taking the form of a hound ❑ *I remembered certain of Bessie's tales, wherein figured a North-of-England spirit, called a 'Gytrash'* (*Jane Eyre* by Charlotte Brontë)

hackney-cabriolet NOUN a two-wheeled carriage with four seats for hire and pulled by a horse ❑ *A hackney-cabriolet was in waiting; with the same vehemence which she had exhibited in addressing Oliver, the girl pulled him in with her, and drew the curtains close.* (*Oliver Twist* by Charles Dickens)

hackney-coach NOUN a four-wheeled horse-drawn vehicle for hire ❑ *The twilight was beginning to close in, when Mr. Brownlow alighted from a hackney-coach at his own door, and knocked softly.* (*Oliver Twist* by Charles Dickens)

haggler NOUN a haggler is someone who travels from place to place selling small goods and items ❑ *when I be plain Jack Durbeyfield, the haggler* (*Tess of the D'Urbervilles* by Thomas Hardy)

halter NOUN a halter is a rope or strap used to lead an animal or to tie it up ❑ *I had of course long been used to a halter and a headstall* (*Black Beauty* by Anna Sewell)

hamlet NOUN a hamlet is a small village or a group of houses in the countryside ❑ *down from the hamlet* (*Treasure Island* by Robert Louis Stevenson)

hand-barrow NOUN a hand-barrow is a device for carrying heavy objects. It is like a wheelbarrow except that it has handles, rather than wheels, for moving the barrow ❑ *his sea chest following behind him in a hand-barrow* (*Treasure Island* by Robert Louis Stevenson)

handspike NOUN a handspike was a stick which was used as a lever ❑ *a bit of stick like a handspike* (*Treasure Island* by Robert Louis Stevenson)

haply ADV haply means by chance or perhaps ❑ *And haply the Queen-Moon is on her throne* (*Ode on a Nightingale* by John Keats)

harem NOUN the harem was the part of the house where the women lived ❑ *mostly they hang round the harem* (*The Adventures of Huckleberry Finn* by Mark Twain)

hautboys NOUN hautboys are oboes ❑ *sausages and puddings resembling flutes and hautboys* (*Gulliver's Travels* by Jonathan Swift)

hawker NOUN a hawker is someone who sells goods to people as he travels rather than from a fixed place like a shop ❑ *to buy some stockings from a hawker* (*Treasure Island* by Robert Louis Stevenson)

hawser NOUN a hawser is a rope used to tie up or tow a ship or boat ❑ *Again among the tiers of shipping, in and out, avoiding rusty chain-cables, frayed hempen hawsers* (*Great Expectations* by Charles Dickens)

headstall NOUN the headstall is the part of the bridle or halter that goes around a horse's head ❑ *I had of course long been used to a halter and a headstall* (*Black Beauty* by Anna Sewell)

hearken VERB hearken means to listen ❑ *though we sometimes stopped to lay hold of each other and hearken* (*Treasure Island* by Robert Louis Stevenson)

heartless ADJ here heartless means without heart or dejected ❑ *I am not heartless* (*The Prelude* by William Wordsworth)

hebdomadal ADJ hebdomadal means weekly ❑ *It was the hebdomadal treat to which we all looked forward from Sabbath to Sabbath* (*Jane Eyre* by Charlotte Brontë)

highwaymen NOUN highwaymen were people who stopped travellers and robbed them ❑ *We are high-waymen* (*The Adventures of Huckleberry Finn* by Mark Twain)

hinds NOUN hinds means farm hands, or people who work on a farm ❑ *He called his hinds about him* (*Gulliver's Travels* by Jonathan Swift)

histrionic ADJ if you refer to someone's behaviour as histrionic, you are being critical of it because it is dramatic and exaggerated ❑ *But the histrionic muse is the darling* (*The Adventures of Huckleberry Finn* by Mark Twain)

hogs NOUN hogs is another word for pigs ❑ *Tom called the hogs 'ingots'* (*The Adventures of Huckleberry Finn* by Mark Twain)

horrors NOUN the horrors are a fit, called delirium tremens, which is caused by drinking too much alcohol ❑ *I'll have the horrors* (*Treasure Island* by Robert Louis Stevenson)

huffy ADJ huffy means to be obviously annoyed or offended about something ❑ *They will feel that more than angry speeches or huffy actions* (*Little Women* by Louisa May Alcott)

hulks NOUN hulks were prison-ships ❑ *The miserable companion of thieves and ruffians, the fallen outcast of low haunts, the associate of the scourings of the jails and hulks* (*Oliver Twist* by Charles Dickens)

humbug NOUN humbug means nonsense or rubbish ❑ *"Bah," said Scrooge. "Humbug!"* (*A Christmas Carol* by Charles Dickens)

humours NOUN it was believed that there were four fluids in the body called humours which decided the temperament of a person depending on how much of each fluid was present ❑ *other peccant humours* (*Gulliver's Travels* by Jonathan Swift)

husbandry NOUN husbandry is farming animals ❑ *bad husbandry were plentifully anointing their wheels* (*Silas Marner* by George Eliot)

huswife NOUN a huswife was a small sewing kit ❑ *but I had put my huswife on it* (*Emma* by Jane Austen)

ideal ADJ ideal in this context means imaginary ❑ *I discovered the yell was not ideal* (*Wuthering Heights* by Emily Brontë)

If our two PHRASE if both our ❑ *If our two loves be one* (*The Good-Morrow* by John Donne)

ignis-fatuus NOUN ignis-fatuus is the light given out by burning marsh gases, which lead careless travellers into danger ❑ *it is madness in all women to let a secret love kindle within them, which, if unreturned and unknown, must devour the life that feeds it; and, if discovered and responded to, must lead ignis-fatuus-like, into miry wilds whence there is no extrication.* (*Jane Eyre* by Charlotte Brontë)

imaginations NOUN here imaginations means schemes or plans ❑ *soon drove out those imaginations* (*Gulliver's Travels* by Jonathan Swift)

impressible ADJ impressible means open or impressionable ❑ *for Marner had one of those impressible, self-doubting natures* (*Silas Marner* by George Eliot)

in good intelligence PHRASE friendly with each other ❑ *that these two persons were in good intelligence with each other* (*Gulliver's Travels* by Jonathan Swift)

inanity NOUN inanity is sillyness or dull stupidity ❑ *Do we not wile away moments of inanity* (*Silas Marner* by George Eliot)

incivility NOUN incivility means rudeness or impoliteness ❑ *if it's only for a piece of incivility like to-night's* (*Treasure Island* by Robert Louis Stevenson)

indigenae NOUN indigenae means natives or people from that area ❑ *an exotic that the surly indigenae will not recognise for kin* (*Wuthering Heights* by Emily Brontë)

indocible ADJ unteachable ❑ *so they were the most restive and indocible* (*Gulliver's Travels* by Jonathan Swift)

ingenuity NOUN inventiveness ❑ *entreated me to give him something as an encouragement to ingenuity* (*Gulliver's Travels* by Jonathan Swift)

ingots NOUN an ingot is a lump of a valuable metal like gold, usually shaped like a brick ❑ *Tom called the hogs 'ingots'* (*The Adventures of Huckleberry Finn* by Mark Twain)

inkstand NOUN an inkstand is a pot which was put on a desk to contain either ink or pencils and pens ❑ *throwing an inkstand at the Lizard as she spoke* (*Alice's Adventures in Wonderland* by Lewis Carroll)

inordinate ADJ without order. To-day inordinate means 'excessive'. ❑ *Though yet untutored and inordinate* (*The Prelude* by William Wordsworth)

intellectuals NOUN here intellectuals means the minds (of the workmen) ❑ *those instructions they give being too refined for the intellectuals of their workmen* (*Gulliver's Travels* by Jonathan Swift)

interview NOUN meeting ❑ *By our first strange and fatal interview* (*On His Mistress* by John Donne)

jacks NOUN jacks are rods for turning a spit over a fire ❑ *It was a small bit of pork suspended from the kettle hanger by a string passed through a large door key, in a way known to primitive housekeepers unpossessed of jacks* (*Silas Marner* by George Eliot)

jews-harp NOUN a jews-harp is a small, metal, musical instrument that is played by the mouth ❑ *A jews-harp's plenty good enough for a rat* (*The Adventures of Huckleberry Finn* by Mark Twain)

jorum NOUN a large bowl ❑ *while Miss Skiffins brewed such a jorum of tea, that the pig in the back premises became strongly excited* (*Great Expectations* by Charles Dickens)

jostled VERB jostled means bumped or pushed by someone or some people

❑ *being jostled himself into the kennel* (*Gulliver's Travels* by Jonathan Swift)

keepsake NOUN a keepsake is a gift which reminds someone of an event or of the person who gave it to them. ❑ *books and ornaments they had in their boudoirs at home: keepsakes that different relations had presented to them* (*Jane Eyre* by Charlotte Brontë)

kenned VERB kenned means knew ❑ *though little kenned the lamplighter that he had any company but Christmas!* (*A Christmas Carol* by Charles Dickens)

kennel NOUN kennel means gutter, which is the edge of a road next to the pavement, where rain water collects and flows away ❑ *being jostled himself into the kennel* (*Gulliver's Travels* by Jonathan Swift)

knock-knee ADJ knock-knee means slanted, at an angle. ❑ *LOT 1 was marked in whitewashed knock-knee letters on the brewhouse* (*Great Expectations* by Charles Dickens)

ladylike ADJ to be ladylike is to behave in a polite, dignified and graceful way ❑ *No, winking isn't ladylike* (*Little Women* by Louisa May Alcott)

lapse NOUN flow ❑ *Stealing with silent lapse to join the brook* (*The Prelude* by William Wordsworth)

larry NOUN larry is an old word which means commotion or noisy celebration ❑ *That was all a part of the larry!* (*Tess of the D'Urbervilles* by Thomas Hardy)

laths NOUN laths are strips of wood ❑ *The panels shrunk, the windows cracked; fragments of plaster fell out of the ceiling, and the naked laths were shown instead* (*A Christmas Carol* by Charles Dickens)

leer NOUN a leer is an unpleasant smile ❑ *with a kind of leer* (*Treasure Island* by Robert Louis Stevenson)

lenitives NOUN these are different kinds of drugs or medicines: lenitives and palliatives were pain relievers; aperitives were laxatives; abstersives caused vomiting; corrosives destroyed human tissue; restringents caused constipation; cephalalgics stopped headaches; icterics were used as medicine for jaundice; apophlegmatics were cough medicine, and acoustics were cures for the loss of hearing ❏ *lenitives, aperitives, abstersives, corrosives, restringents, palliatives, laxatives, cephalalgics, icterics, apophlegmatics, acoustics* (*Gulliver's Travels* by Jonathan Swift)

lest CONJ in case. If you do something lest something (usually) unpleasant happens you do it to try to prevent it happening ❏ *She went in without knocking, and hurried upstairs, in great fear lest she should meet the real Mary Ann* (*Alice's Adventures in Wonderland* by Lewis Carroll)

levee NOUN a levee is an old term for a meeting held in the morning, shortly after the person holding the meeting has got out of bed ❏ *I used to attend the King's levee once or twice a week* (*Gulliver's Travels* by Jonathan Swift)

life-preserver NOUN a club which had lead inside it to make it heavier and therefore more dangerous ❏ *and with no more suspicious articles displayed to view than two or three heavy bludgeons which stood in a corner, and a 'life-preserver' that hung over the chimney-piece.* (*Oliver Twist* by Charles Dickens)

lighterman NOUN a lighterman is another word for sailor ❏ *in and out, hammers going in ship-builders' yards, saws going at timber, clashing engines going at things unknown, pumps going in leaky ships, capstans going, ships going out to sea, and unintelligible sea creatures roaring curses over the bulwarks at respondent lightermen* (*Great Expectations* by Charles Dickens)

livery NOUN servants often wore a uniform known as a livery ❏ *suddenly a footman in livery came running out of the wood* (*Alice's Adventures in Wonderland* by Lewis Carroll)

livid ADJ livid means pale or ash coloured. Livid also means very angry ❏ *a dirty, livid white* (*Treasure Island* by Robert Louis Stevenson)

lottery-tickets NOUN a popular card game ❏ *and Mrs. Philips protested that they would have a nice comfortable noisy game of lottery tickets* (*Pride and Prejudice* by Jane Austen)

lower and upper world PHRASE the earth and the heavens are the lower and upper worlds ❏ *the changes in the lower and upper world* (*Gulliver's Travels* by Jonathan Swift)

lustres NOUN lustres are chandeliers. A chandelier is a large, decorative frame which holds light bulbs or candles and hangs from the ceiling ❏ *the lustres, lights, the carving and the guilding* (*The Prelude* by William Wordsworth)

lynched VERB killed without a criminal trial by a crowd of people ❏ *He'll never know how nigh he come to getting lynched* (*The Adventures of Huckleberry Finn* by Mark Twain)

malingering VERB if someone is malingering they are pretending to be ill to avoid working ❏ *And you stand there malingering* (*Treasure Island* by Robert Louis Stevenson)

managing PHRASE treating with consideration ❏ *to think the honour of my own kind not worth managing* (*Gulliver's Travels* by Jonathan Swift)

manhood PHRASE manhood means human nature ❏ *concerning the nature of manhood* (*Gulliver's Travels* by Jonathan Swift)

man-trap NOUN a man-trap is a set of steel jaws that snap shut when trodden on and trap a person's leg

❏ *"Don't go to him,"* I called out of
the window, *"he's an assassin! A
man-trap!"* (*Oliver Twist* by
Charles Dickens)

maps NOUN charts of the night sky ❏
*Let maps to others, worlds on worlds
have shown* (*The Good-Morrow* by
John Donne)

mark VERB look at or notice ❏ *Mark
but this flea, and mark in this* (*The
Flea* by John Donne)

maroons NOUN A maroon is someone
who has been left in a place which
it is difficult for them to escape
from, like a small island ❏ *if
schooners, islands, and maroons*
(*Treasure Island* by Robert Louis
Stevenson)

mast NOUN here mast means the fruit
of forest trees ❏ *a quantity of
acorns, dates, chestnuts, and other
mast* (*Gulliver's Travels* by Jonathan
Swift)

mate VERB defeat ❏ *Where Mars did
mate the warlike Carthigens* (*Doctor
Faustus Chorus* by Christopher
Marlowe)

mealy ADJ Mealy when used to describe
a face meant palid, pale or colourless
❏ *I only know two sorts of boys.
Mealy boys, and beef-faced boys*
(*Oliver Twist* by Charles Dickens)

middling ADJ fairly or moderately
❏ *she worked me middling hard for
about an hour* (*The Adventures of
Huckleberry Finn* by Mark Twain)

mill NOUN a mill, or treadmill, was a
device for hard labour or punishment in prison ❏ *Was you never on
the mill?* (*Oliver Twist* by Charles
Dickens)

milliner's shop NOUN a milliner's sold
fabrics, clothing, lace and accesso-
ries; as time went on they special-
ized more and more in hats ❏ *to
pay their duty to their aunt and to a
milliner's shop just over the way*
(*Pride and Prejudice* by Jane Austen)

minching un' munching PHRASE how
people in the north of England
used to describe the way people

from the south speak ❏ *Minching
un' munching!* (*Wuthering Heights*
by Emily Brontë)

mine NOUN gold ❏ *Whether both
th'Indias of spice and mine* (*The
Sun Rising* by John Donne)

mire NOUN mud ❏ *'Tis my fate to be
always ground into the mire under
the iron heel of oppression* (*The
Adventures of Huckleberry Finn* by
Mark Twain)

miscellany NOUN a miscellany is a
collection of many different kinds
of things ❏ *under that, the miscellany began* (*Treasure Island* by
Robert Louis Stevenson)

mistarshers NOUN mistarshers means
moustache, which is the hair that
grows on a man's upper lip ❏ *when
he put his hand up to his mistarshers* (*Tess of the D'Urbervilles* by
Thomas Hardy)

morrow NOUN here good-morrow
means tomorrow and a new and
better life ❏ *And now good-morrow
to our waking souls* (*The Good-
Morrow* by John Donne)

mortification NOUN mortification is an
old word for gangrene which is
when part of the body decays or
'dies' because of disease ❏ *Yes, it
was a mortification–that was it*
(*The Adventures of Huckleberry
Finn* by Mark Twain)

mought PARTICIPLE mought is an old
spelling of might ❏ *what you
mought call me? You mought call
me captain* (*Treasure Island* by
Robert Louis Stevenson)

move VERB move me not means do not
make me angry ❏ *Move me not,
Faustus* (*Doctor Faustus 2.1* by
Christopher Marlowe)

muffin-cap NOUN a muffin cap is a flat
cap made from wool ❏ *the old one,
remained stationary in the muffin-
cap and leathers* (*Oliver Twist* by
Charles Dickens)

mulatter NOUN a mulatter was another
word for mulatto, which is a person
with parents who are from different

races ❑ *a mulatter, most as white as a white man* (*The Adventures of Huckleberry Finn* by Mark Twain)

mummery NOUN mummery is an old word that meant meaningless (or pretentious) ceremony ❑ *When they were all gone, and when Trabb and his men–but not his boy: I looked for him–had crammed their mummery into bags, and were gone too, the house felt wholesomer.* (*Great Expectations* by Charles Dickens)

nap NOUN the nap is the woolly surface on a new item of clothing. Here the surface has been worn away so it looks bare ❑ *like an old hat with the nap rubbed off* (*The Adventures of Huckleberry Finn* by Mark Twain)

natural ■ NOUN a natural is a person born with learning difficulties ❑ *though he had been left to his particular care by their deceased father, who thought him almost a natural.* (*David Copperfield* by Charles Dickens) ■ ADJ natural meant illegitimate ❑ *Harriet Smith was the natural daughter of somebody* (*Emma* by Jane Austen)

navigator NOUN a navigator was originally someone employed to dig canals. It is the origin of the word 'navvy' meaning a labourer ❑ *She ascertained from me in a few words what it was all about, comforted Dora, and gradually convinced her that I was not a labourer–from my manner of stating the case I believe Dora concluded that I was a navigator, and went balancing myself up and down a plank all day with a wheelbarrow–and so brought us together in peace.* (*David Copperfield* by Charles Dickens)

necromancy NOUN necromancy means a kind of magic where the magician speaks to spirits or ghosts to find out what will happen in the future ❑ *He surfeits upon cursed necromancy* (*Doctor Faustus chorus* by Christopher Marlowe)

negus NOUN a negus is a hot drink made from sweetened wine and water ❑ *He sat placidly perusing the newspaper, with his little head on one side, and a glass of warm sherry negus at his elbow.* (*David Copperfield* by Charles Dickens)

nice ADJ discriminating. Able to make good judgements or choices ❑ *consequently a claim to be nice* (*Emma* by Jane Austen)

nigh ADV nigh means near ❑ *He'll never know how nigh he come to getting lynched* (*The Adventures of Huckleberry Finn* by Mark Twain)

nimbleness NOUN nimbleness means being able to move very quickly or skillfully ❑ *and with incredible accuracy and nimbleness* (*Treasure Island* by Robert Louis Stevenson)

noggin NOUN a noggin is a small mug or a wooden cup ❑ *you'll bring me one noggin of rum* (*Treasure Island* by Robert Louis Stevenson)

none ADJ neither ❑ *none can die* (*The Good-Morrow* by John Donne)

notices NOUN observations ❑ *Arch are his notices* (*The Prelude* by William Wordsworth)

occiput NOUN occiput means the back of the head ❑ *saw off the occiput of each couple* (*Gulliver's Travels* by Jonathan Swift)

officiously ADJ kindly ❑ *the governess who attended Glumdalclitch very officiously lifted me up* (*Gulliver's Travels* by Jonathan Swift)

old salt PHRASE old salt is a slang term for an experienced sailor ❑ *a 'true sea-dog', and a 'real old salt'* (*Treasure Island* by Robert Louis Stevenson)

or ere PHRASE before ❑ *or ere the Hall was built* (*The Prelude* by William Wordsworth)

ostler NOUN one who looks after horses at an inn ❑ *The bill paid, and the waiter remembered, and the ostler not forgotten, and the chambermaid taken into* consideration (*Great Expectations* by Charles Dickens)

ostry NOUN an ostry is an old word for a pub or hotel ❑ *lest I send you into the ostry with a vengeance* (*Doctor Faustus 2.2* by Christopher Marlowe)

outrunning the constable PHRASE outrunning the constable meant spending more than you earn ❑ *but I shall by this means be able to check your bills and to pull you up if I find you outrunning the constable.* (*Great Expectations* by Charles Dickens)

over ADJ across ❑ *It is in length six yards, and in the thickest part at least three yards over* (*Gulliver's Travels* by Jonathan Swift)

over the broomstick PHRASE this is a phrase meaning 'getting married without a formal ceremony' ❑ *They both led tramping lives, and this woman in Gerrard-street here, had been married very young, over the broomstick (as we say), to a tramping man, and was a perfect fury in point of jealousy.* (*Great Expectations* by Charles Dickens)

own VERB own means to admit or to acknowledge ❑ *It's my old girl that advises. She has the head. But I never own to it before her. Discipline must be maintained* (*Bleak House* by Charles Dickens)

page NOUN here page means a boy employed to run errands ❑ *not my feigned page* (*On His Mistress* by John Donne)

paid pretty dear PHRASE paid pretty dear means paid a high price or suffered quite a lot ❑ *I paid pretty dear for my monthly fourpenny piece* (*Treasure Island* by Robert Louis Stevenson)

pannikins NOUN pannikins were small tin cups ❑ *of lifting light glasses and cups to his lips, as if they were clumsy pannikins* (*Great Expectations* by Charles Dickens)

pards NOUN pards are leopards ❑ *Not*

charioted by Bacchus and his pards (*Ode on a Nightingale* by John Keats)

parlour boarder NOUN a pupil who lived with the family ❑ *and somebody had lately raised her from the condition of scholar to parlour boarder* (*Emma* by Jane Austen)

particular, a London PHRASE London in Victorian times and up to the 1950s was famous for having very dense fog–which was a combination of real fog and the smog of pollution from factories ❑ *This is a London particular . . . A fog, miss'* (*Bleak House* by Charles Dickens)

patten NOUN pattens were wooden soles which were fixed to shoes by straps to protect the shoes in wet weather ❑ *carrying a basket like the Great Seal of England in plaited straw, a pair of pattens, a spare shawl, and an umbrella, though it was a fine bright day* (*Great Expectations* by Charles Dickens)

paviour NOUN a paviour was a labourer who worked on the street pavement ❑ *the paviour his pickaxe* (*Oliver Twist* by Charles Dickens)

peccant ADJ peccant means unhealthy ❑ *other peccant humours* (*Gulliver's Travels* by Jonathan Swift)

penetralium NOUN penetralium is a word used to describe the inner rooms of the house ❑ *and I had no desire to aggravate his impatience previous to inspecting the penetralium* (*Wuthering Heights* by Emily Brontë)

pensive ADV pensive means deep in thought or thinking seriously about something ❑ *and she was leaning pensive on a tomb-stone on her right elbow* (*The Adventures of Huckleberry Finn* by Mark Twain)

penury NOUN penury is the state of being extremely poor ❑ *Distress, if not penury, loomed in the distance* (*Tess of the D'Urbervilles* by Thomas Hardy)

perspective NOUN telescope ❑ *a pocket perspective* (*Gulliver's Travels* by Jonathan Swift)

phaeton NOUN a phaeton was an open carriage for four people ❑ *often condescends to drive by my humble abode in her little phaeton and ponies* (Pride and Prejudice by Jane Austen)

phantasm NOUN a phantasm is an illusion, something that is not real. It is sometimes used to mean ghost ❑ *Experience had bred no fancies in him that could raise the phantasm of appetite* (Silas Marner by George Eliot)

physic NOUN here physic means medicine ❑ *there I studied physic two years and seven months* (Gulliver's Travels by Jonathan Swift)

pinioned VERB to pinion is to hold both arms so that a person cannot move them ❑ *But the relentless Ghost pinioned him in both his arms, and forced him to observe what happened next.* (A Christmas Carol by Charles Dickens)

piquet NOUN piquet was a popular card game in the C18th ❑ *Mr Hurst and Mr Bingley were at piquet* (Pride and Prejudice by Jane Austen)

plaister NOUN a plaister is a piece of cloth on which an apothecary (or pharmacist) would spread ointment. The cloth is then applied to wounds or bruises to treat them ❑ *Then, she gave the knife a final smart wipe on the edge of the plaister, and then sawed a very thick round off the loaf: which she finally, before separating from the loaf, hewed into two halves, of which Joe got one, and I the other.* (Great Expectations by Charles Dickens)

plantations NOUN here plantations means colonies, which are countries controlled by a more powerful country ❑ *besides our plantations in America* (Gulliver's Travels by Jonathan Swift)

plastic ADV here plastic is an old term meaning shaping or a power that was forming ❑ *A plastic power abode with me* (The Prelude by William Wordsworth)

players NOUN actors ❑ *of players which upon the world's stage be* (On His Mistress by John Donne)

plump ADV all at once, suddenly ❑ *But it took a bit of time to get it well round, the change come so uncommon plump, didn't it?* (Great Expectations by Charles Dickens)

plundered VERB to plunder is to rob or steal from ❑ *These crosses stand for the names of ships or towns that they sank or plundered* (Treasure Island by Robert Louis Stevenson)

pommel ■ VERB to pommel someone is to hit them repeatedly with your fists ❑ *hug him round the neck, pommel his back, and kick his legs in irrepressible affection!* (A Christmas Carol by Charles Dickens) ■ NOUN a pommel is the part of a saddle that rises up at the front ❑ *He had his gun across his pommel* (The Adventures of Huckleberry Finn by Mark Twain)

poor's rates NOUN poor's rates were property taxes which were used to support the poor ❑ *"Oh!" replied the undertaker; "why, you know, Mr. Bumble, I pay a good deal towards the poor's rates."* (Oliver Twist by Charles Dickens)

popular ADJ popular means ruled by the people, or Republican, rather than ruled by a monarch ❑ *With those of Greece compared and popular Rome* (The Prelude by William Wordsworth)

porringer NOUN a porringer is a small bowl ❑ *Of this festive composition each boy had one porringer, and no more* (Oliver Twist by Charles Dickens)

postboy NOUN a postboy was the driver of a horse-drawn carriage ❑ *He spoke to a postboy who was dozing under the gateway* (Oliver Twist by Charles Dickens)

post-chaise NOUN a fast carriage for two or four passengers ❑ *Looking round, he saw that it was a post-chaise, driven at great speed* (Oliver Twist by Charles Dickens)

postern NOUN a small gate usually at the back of a building ❏ *The little servant happening to be entering the fortress with two hot rolls, I passed through the postern and crossed the drawbridge, in her company* (*Great Expectations* by Charles Dickens)

pottle NOUN a pottle was a small basket ❏ *He had a paper-bag under each arm and a pottle of strawberries in one hand . . .* (*Great Expectations* by Charles Dickens)

pounce NOUN pounce is a fine powder used to prevent ink spreading on untreated paper ❏ *in that grim atmosphere of pounce and parchment, red-tape, dusty wafers, ink-jars, brief and draft paper, law reports, writs, declarations, and bills of costs* (*David Copperfield* by Charles Dickens)

pox NOUN pox means sexually transmitted diseases like syphilis ❏ *how the pox in all its consequences and denominations* (*Gulliver's Travels* by Jonathan Swift)

prelibation NOUN prelibation means a foretaste of or an example of something to come ❏ *A prelibation to the mower's scythe* (*The Prelude* by William Wordsworth)

prentice NOUN an apprentice ❏ *and Joe, sitting on an old gun, had told me that when I was 'prentice to him regularly bound, we would have such Larks there!* (*Great Expectations* by Charles Dickens)

presently ADV immediately ❏ *I presently knew what they meant* (*Gulliver's Travels* by Jonathan Swift)

pumpion NOUN pumpkin ❏ *for it was almost as large as a small pumpion* (*Gulliver's Travels* by Jonathan Swift)

punctual ADJ kept in one place ❏ *was not a punctual presence, but a spirit* (*The Prelude* by William Wordsworth)

quadrille ■ NOUN a quadrille is a dance invented in France which is usually performed by four couples ❏ *However, Mr Swiveller had Miss Sophy's hand for the first quadrille (country-dances being low, were utterly proscribed)* (*The Old Curiosity Shop* by Charles Dickens) ■ NOUN quadrille was a card game for four people ❏ *to make up her pool of quadrille in the evening* (*Pride and Prejudice* by Jane Austen)

quality NOUN gentry or upper-class people ❏ *if you are with the quality* (*The Adventures of Huckleberry Finn* by Mark Twain)

quick parts PHRASE quick-witted ❏ *Mr Bennet was so odd a mixture of quick parts* (*Pride and Prejudice* by Jane Austen)

quid NOUN a quid is something chewed or kept in the mouth, like a piece of tobacco ❏ *rolling his quid* (*Treasure Island* by Robert Louis Stevenson)

quit VERB quit means to avenge or to make even ❏ *But Faustus's death shall quit my infamy* (*Doctor Faustus 4.3* by Christopher Marlowe)

rags NOUN divisions ❏ *Nor hours, days, months, which are the rags of time* (*The Sun Rising* by John Donne)

raiment NOUN raiment means clothing ❏ *the mountain shook off turf and flower, had only heath for raiment and crag for gem* (*Jane Eyre* by Charlotte Brontë)

rain cats and dogs PHRASE an expression meaning rain heavily. The origin of the expression is unclear ❏ *But it'll perhaps rain cats and dogs to-morrow* (*Silas Marner* by George Eliot)

raised Cain PHRASE raised Cain means caused a lot of trouble. Cain is a character in the Bible who killed his brother Abel ❏ *and every time he got drunk he raised Cain around town* (*The Adventures of Huckleberry Finn* by Mark Twain)

rambling ADJ rambling means confused and not very clear ❏ *my* *head began to be filled very early with rambling thoughts* (*Robinson Crusoe* by Daniel Defoe)

raree-show NOUN a raree-show is an old term for a peep-show or a fair-ground entertainment ❑ *A raree-show is here, with children gathered round* (*The Prelude* by William Wordsworth)

recusants NOUN people who resisted authority ❑ *hardy recusants* (*The Prelude* by William Wordsworth)

redounding VERB eddying. An eddy is a movement in water or air which goes round and round instead of flowing in one direction ❑ *mists and steam-like fogs redounding everywhere* (*The Prelude* by William Wordsworth)

redundant ADJ here redundant means overflowing but Wordsworth also uses it to mean excessively large or too big ❑ *A tempest, a redundant energy* (*The Prelude* by William Wordsworth)

reflex NOUN reflex is a shortened version of reflexion, which is an alternative spelling of reflection ❑ *To cut across the reflex of a star* (*The Prelude* by William Wordsworth)

Reformatory NOUN a prison for young offenders/criminals ❑ *Even when I was taken to have a new suit of clothes, the tailor had orders to make them like a kind of Reformatory, and on no account to let me have the free use of my limbs.* (*Great Expectations* by Charles Dickens)

remorse NOUN pity or compassion ❑ *by that remorse* (*On His Mistress* by John Donne)

render VERB in this context render means give. ❑ *and Sarah could render no reason that would be sanctioned by the feeling of the community.* (*Silas Marner* by George Eliot)

repeater NOUN a repeater was a watch that chimed the last hour when a button was pressed–as a result it was useful in the dark ❑ *And his watch is a gold repeater, and worth a hundred pound if it's worth a penny.* (*Great Expectations* by Charles Dickens)

repugnance NOUN repugnance means a strong dislike of something or someone ❑ *overcoming a strong repugnance* (*Treasure Island* by Robert Louis Stevenson)

reverence NOUN reverence means bow. When you bow to someone, you briefly bend your body towards them as a formal way of showing them respect ❑ *made my reverence* (*Gulliver's Travels* by Jonathan Swift)

reverie NOUN a reverie is a day dream ❑ *I can guess the subject of your reverie* (*Pride and Prejudice* by Jane Austen)

revival NOUN a religious meeting held in public ❑ *well I'd ben a-running' a little temperance revival thar' bout a week* (*The Adventures of Huckleberry Finn* by Mark Twain)

revolt VERB revolt means turn back or stop your present course of action and go back to what you were doing before ❑ *Revolt, or I'll in piecemeal tear thy flesh* (*Doctor Faustus 5.1* by Christopher Marlowe)

rheumatics/rheumatism NOUN rheumatics [rheumatism] is an illness that makes your joints or muscles stiff and painful ❑ *a new cure for the rheumatics* (*Treasure Island* by Robert Louis Stevenson)

riddance NOUN riddance is usually used in the form good riddance which you say when you are pleased that something has gone or been left behind ❑ *I'd better go into the house, and die and be a riddance* (*David Copperfield* by Charles Dickens)

rimy ADJ rimy is an ADJECTIVE which means covered in ice or frost ❑ *It was a rimy morning, and very damp* (*Great Expectations* by Charles Dickens)

riper ADJ riper means more mature or older ❑ *At riper years to Wittenberg he went* (*Doctor Faustus chorus* by Christopher Marlowe)

rubber NOUN a set of games in whist or backgammon ❑ *her father was sure of his rubber* (*Emma* by Jane Austen)

ruffian NOUN a ruffian is a person who behaves violently ❑ *and when the ruffian had told him* (*Treasure Island* by Robert Louis Stevenson)

sadness NOUN sadness is an old term meaning seriousness ❑ *But I prithee tell me, in good sadness* (*Doctor Faustus 2.2* by Christopher Marlowe)

sailed before the mast PHRASE this phrase meant someone who did not look like a sailor ❑ *he had none of the appearance of a man that sailed before the mast* (*Treasure Island* by Robert Louis Stevenson)

scabbard NOUN a scabbard is the covering for a sword or dagger ❑ *Girded round its middle was an antique scabbard; but no sword was in it, and the ancient sheath was eaten up with rust* (*A Christmas Carol* by Charles Dickens)

schooners NOUN A schooner is a fast, medium-sized sailing ship ❑ *if schooners, islands, and maroons* (*Treasure Island* by Robert Louis Stevenson)

science NOUN learning or knowledge ❑ *Even Science, too, at hand* (*The Prelude* by William Wordsworth)

scrouge VERB to scrouge means to squeeze or to crowd ❑ *to scrouge in and get a sight* (*The Adventures of Huckleberry Finn* by Mark Twain)

scrutore NOUN a scrutore, or escritoire, was a writing table ❑ *set me gently on my feet upon the scrutore* (*Gulliver's Travels* by Jonathan Swift)

scutcheon/escutcheon NOUN an escutcheon is a shield with a coat of arms, or the symbols of a family name, engraved on it ❑ *On the scutcheon we'll have a bend* (*The*

Adventures of Huckleberry Finn by Mark Twain)

sea-dog PHRASE sea-dog is a slang term for an experienced sailor or pirate ❑ *a 'true sea-dog', and a 'real old salt,'* (*Treasure Island* by Robert Louis Stevenson)

see the lions PHRASE to see the lions was to go and see the sights of London. Originally the phrase referred to the menagerie in the Tower of London and later in Regent's Park ❑ *We will go and see the lions for an hour or two–it's something to have a fresh fellow like you to show them to, Copperfield* (*David Copperfield* by Charles Dickens)

self-conceit NOUN self-conceit is an old term which means having too high an opinion of oneself, or deceiving yourself ❑ *Till swollen with cunning, of a self-conceit* (*Doctor Faustus chorus* by Christopher Marlowe)

seneschal NOUN a steward ❑ *where a grey-headed seneschal sings a funny chorus with a funnier body of vassals* (*Oliver Twist* by Charles Dickens)

sensible ADJ if you were sensible of something you are aware or conscious of something ❑ *If my children are silly I must hope to be always sensible of it* (*Pride and Prejudice* by Jane Austen)

sessions NOUN court cases were heard at specific times of the year called sessions ❑ *He lay in prison very ill, during the whole interval between his committal for trial, and the coming round of the Sessions.* (*Great Expectations* by Charles Dickens)

shabby ADJ shabby places look old and in bad condition ❑ *a little bit of a shabby village named Pikesville* (*The Adventures of Huckleberry Finn* by Mark Twain)

shay-cart NOUN a shay-cart was a small cart drawn by one horse ❑ *"I were at the Bargemen t'other night, Pip;"*

whenever he subsided into affection, he called me Pip, and whenever he relapsed into politeness he called me Sir; "when there come up in his shay-cart Pumblechook." (*Great Expectations* by Charles Dickens)

shilling NOUN a shilling is an old unit of currency. There were twenty shillings in every British pound ❏ *"Ten shillings too much," said the gentleman in the white waistcoat.* (*Oliver Twist* by Charles Dickens)

shines NOUN tricks or games ❏ *well, it would make a cow laugh to see the shines that old idiot cut* (*The Adventures of Huckleberry Finn* by Mark Twain)

shirking VERB shirking means not doing what you are meant to be doing, or evading your duties ❏ *some of you shirking lubbers* (*Treasure Island* by Robert Louis Stevenson)

shiver my timbers PHRASE shiver my timbers is an expression which was used by sailors and pirates to express surprise ❏ *why, shiver my timbers, if I hadn't forgotten my score!* (*Treasure Island* by Robert Louis Stevenson)

shoe-roses NOUN shoe-roses were roses made from ribbons which were stuck on to shoes as decoration ❏ *the very shoe-roses for Netherfield were got by proxy* (*Pride and Prejudice* by Jane Austen)

singular ADJ singular means very great and remarkable or strange ❏ *"Singular dream," he says* (*The Adventures of Huckleberry Finn* by Mark Twain)

sire NOUN sire is an old word which means lord or master or elder ❏ *She also defied her sire* (*Little Women* by Louisa May Alcott)

sixpence NOUN a sixpence was half of a shilling ❏ *if she had only a shilling in the world, she would be very likely to give away sixpence of it* (*Emma* by Jane Austen)

slavey NOUN the word slavey was used when there was only one servant in a house or boarding-house–so she had to perform all the duties of a larger staff ❏ *Two distinct knocks, sir, will produce the slavey at any time* (*The Old Curiosity Shop* by Charles Dickens)

slender ADJ weak ❏ *In slender accents of sweet verse* (*The Prelude* by William Wordsworth)

slop-shops NOUN slop-shops were shops where cheap ready-made clothes were sold. They mainly sold clothes to sailors ❏ *Accordingly, I took the jacket off, that I might learn to do without it; and carrying it under my arm, began a tour of inspection of the various slop-shops.* (*David Copperfield* by Charles Dickens)

sluggard NOUN a lazy person ❏ *"Stand up and repeat 'Tis the voice of the sluggard,'" said the Gryphon.* (*Alice's Adventures in Wonderland* by Lewis Carroll)

smallpox NOUN smallpox is a serious infectious disease ❏ *by telling the men we had smallpox aboard* (*The Adventures of Huckleberry Finn* by Mark Twain)

smalls NOUN smalls are short trousers ❏ *It is difficult for a large-headed, small-eyed youth, of lumbering make and heavy countenance, to look dignified under any circumstances; but it is more especially so, when superadded to these personal attractions are a red nose and yellow smalls* (*Oliver Twist* by Charles Dickens)

sneeze-box NOUN a box for snuff was called a sneeze-box because sniffing snuff makes the user sneeze ❏ *To think of Jack Dawkins — lummy Jack — the Dodger — the Artful Dodger — going abroad for a common twopenny-halfpenny sneeze-box!* (*Oliver Twist* by Charles Dickens)

snorted VERB slept ❏ *Or snorted we in the Seven Sleepers' den?* (*The Good-Morrow* by John Donne)

snuff NOUN snuff is tobacco in powder form which is taken by sniffing ❏

as he thrust his thumb and fore-finger into the proffered snuff-box of the undertaker: which was an ingenious little model of a patent coffin. (*Oliver Twist* by Charles Dickens)

soliloquized VERB to soliloquize is when an actor in a play speaks to himself or herself rather than to another actor ❑ *"A new servitude! There is something in that," I soliloquized (mentally, be it understood; I did not talk aloud)* (*Jane Eyre* by Charlotte Brontë)

sough NOUN a sough is a drain or a ditch ❑ *as you may have noticed the sough that runs from the marshes* (*Wuthering Heights* by Emily Brontë)

spirits NOUN a spirit is the nonphysical part of a person which is believed to remain alive after their death ❑ *that I might raise up spirits when I please* (*Doctor Faustus 1.5* by Christopher Marlowe)

spleen ■ NOUN here spleen means a type of sadness or depression which was thought to only affect the wealthy ❑ *yet here I could plainly discover the true seeds of spleen* (*Gulliver's Travels* by Jonathan Swift) ■ NOUN irritability and low spirits ❑ *Adieu to disappointment and spleen* (*Pride and Prejudice* by Jane Austen)

spondulicks NOUN spondulicks is a slang word which means money ❑ *not for all his spondulicks and as much more on top of it* (*The Adventures of Huckleberry Finn* by Mark Twain)

stalled of VERB to be stalled of something is to be bored with it ❑ *I'm stalled of doing naught* (*Wuthering Heights* by Emily Brontë)

stanchion NOUN a stanchion is a pole or bar that stands upright and is used as a buidling support ❑ *and slid down a stanchion* (*The Adventures of Huckleberry Finn* by Mark Twain)

stang NOUN stang is another word for pole which was an old measurement ❑ *These fields were intermingled*

with woods of half a stang (*Gulliver's Travels* by Jonathan Swift)

starlings NOUN a starling is a wall built around the pillars that support a bridge to protect the pillars ❑ *There were states of the tide when, having been down the river, I could not get back through the eddy-chafed arches and starlings of old London Bridge* (*Great Expectations* by Charles Dickens)

startings NOUN twitching or night-time movements of the body ❑ *with midnight's startings* (*On His Mistress* by John Donne)

stomacher NOUN a panel at the front of a dress ❑ *but send her aunt the pattern of a stomacher* (*Emma* by Jane Austen)

stoop VERB swoop ❑ *Once a kite hovering over the garden made a swoop at me* (*Gulliver's Travels* by Jonathan Swift)

succedaneum NOUN a succedaneum is a substitute ❑ *But as a succedaneum* (*The Prelude* by William Wordsworth)

suet NOUN a hard animal fat used in cooking ❑ *and your jaws are too weak For anything tougher than suet* (*Alice's Adventures in Wonderland* by Lewis Carroll)

sultry ADJ sultry weather is hot and damp. Here sultry means unpleasant or risky ❑ *for it was getting pretty sultry for us* (*The Adventures of Huckleberry Finn* by Mark Twain)

summerset NOUN summerset is an old spelling of somersault. If someone does a somersault, they turn over completely in the air ❑ *I have seen him do the summerset* (*Gulliver's Travels* by Jonathan Swift)

supper NOUN supper was a light meal taken late in the evening. The main meal was dinner which was eaten at four or five in the afternoon ❑ *and the supper table was all set out* (*Emma* by Jane Austen)

surfeits VERB to surfeit in something is to have far too much of it, or to overindulge in it to an unhealthy degree ❑ *He surfeits upon cursed necromancy* (*Doctor Faustus chorus* by Christopher Marlowe)

surtout NOUN a surtout is a long close-fitting overcoat ❑ *He wore a long black surtout reaching nearly to his ankles* (*The Old Curiosity Shop* by Charles Dickens)

swath NOUN swath is the width of corn cut by a scythe ❑ *while thy hook Spares the next swath* (*Ode to Autumn* by John Keats)

sylvan ADJ sylvan means belonging to the woods ❑ *Sylvan historian* (*Ode on a Grecian Urn* by John Keats)

taction NOUN taction means touch. This means that the people had to be touched on the mouth or the ears to get their attention ❑ *without being roused by some external taction upon the organs of speech and hearing* (*Gulliver's Travels* by Jonathan Swift)

Tag and Rag and Bobtail PHRASE the riff-raff, or lower classes. Used in an insulting way ❑ *"No," said he; "not till it got about that there was no protection on the premises, and it come to be considered dangerous, with convicts and Tag and Rag and Bobtail going up and down."* (*Great Expectations* by Charles Dickens)

tallow NOUN tallow is hard animal fat that is used to make candles and soap ❑ *and a lot of tallow candles* (*The Adventures of Huckleberry Finn* by Mark Twain)

tan VERB to tan means to beat or whip ❑ *and if I catch you about that school I'll tan you good* (*The Adventures of Huckleberry Finn* by Mark Twain)

tanyard NOUN the tanyard is part of a tannery, which is a place where leather is made from animal skins ❑ *hid in the old tanyard* (*The Adventures of Huckleberry Finn* by Mark Twain)

tarry ADJ tarry means the colour of tar or black ❑ *his tarry pig-tail* (*Treasure Island* by Robert Louis Stevenson)

thereof PHRASE from there ❑ *By all desires which thereof did ensue* (*On His Mistress* by John Donne)

thick with, be PHRASE if you are 'thick with someone' you are very close, sharing secrets–it is often used to describe people who are planning something secret ❑ *Hasn't he been thick with Mr Heathcliff lately?* (*Wuthering Heights* by Emily Brontë)

thimble NOUN a thimble is a small cover used to protect the finger while sewing ❑ *The paper had been sealed in several places by a thimble* (*Treasure Island* by Robert Louis Stevenson)

thirtover ADJ thirtover is an old word which means obstinate or that someone is very determined to do want they want and can not be persuaded to do something in another way ❑ *I have been living on in a thirtover, lackadaisical way* (*Tess of the D'Urbervilles* by Thomas Hardy)

timbrel NOUN timbrel is a tambourine ❑ *What pipes and timbrels?* (*Ode on a Grecian Urn* by John Keats)

tin NOUN tin is slang for money/cash ❑ *Then the plain question is, an't it a pity that this state of things should continue, and how much better would it be for the old gentleman to hand over a reasonable amount of tin, and make it all right and comfortable* (*The Old Curiosity Shop* by Charles Dickens)

tincture NOUN a tincture is a medicine made with alcohol and a small amount of a drug ❑ *with ink composed of a cephalic tincture* (*Gulliver's Travels* by Jonathan Swift)

tithe NOUN a tithe is a tax paid to the church ❑ *and held farms which, speaking from a spiritual point of view, paid highly-desirable tithes* (*Silas Marner* by George Eliot)

towardly ADJ a towardly child is dutiful or obedient ❏ *and a towardly child* (*Gulliver's Travels* by Jonathan Swift)

toys NOUN trifles are things which are considered to have little importance, value, or significance ❏ *purchase my life from them by some bracelets, glass rings, and other toys* (*Gulliver's Travels* by Jonathan Swift)

tract NOUN a tract is a religious pamphlet or leaflet ❏ *and Joe Harper got a hymn-book and a tract* (*The Adventures of Huckleberry Finn* by Mark Twain)

train-oil NOUN train-oil is oil from whale blubber ❏ *The train-oil and gunpowder were shoved out of sight in a minute* (*Wuthering Heights* by Emily Brontë)

tribulation NOUN tribulation means the suffering or difficulty you experience in a particular situation ❏ *Amy was learning this distinction through much tribulation* (*Little Women* by Louisa May Alcott)

trivet NOUN a trivet is a three-legged stand for resting a pot or kettle ❏ *a pocket-knife in his right; and a pewter pot on the trivet* (*Oliver Twist* by Charles Dickens)

trot line NOUN a trot line is a fishing line to which a row of smaller fishing lines are attached ❏ *when he got along I was hard at it taking up a trot line* (*The Adventures of Huckleberry Finn* by Mark Twain)

troth NOUN oath or pledge ❏ *I wonder, by my troth* (*The Good-Morrow* by John Donne)

truckle NOUN a truckle bedstead is a bed that is on wheels and can be slid under another bed to save space ❏ *It rose under my hand, and the door yielded. Looking in, I saw a lighted candle on a table, a bench, and a mattress on a truckle bedstead.* (*Great Expectations* by Charles Dickens)

trump NOUN a trump is a good, reliable person wo can be trusted ❏ *This lad Hawkins is a trump, I perceive* (*Treasure Island* by Robert Louis Stevenson)

tucker NOUN a tucker is a frilly lace collar which is worn around the neck ❏ *Whereat Scrooge's niece's sister‾the plump one with the lace tucker: not the one with the roses‾blushed.* (*A Christmas Carol* by Charles Dickens)

tureen NOUN a large bowl with a lid from which soup or vegetables are served ❏ *Waiting in a hot tureen!* (*Alice's Adventures in Wonderland* by Lewis Carroll)

turnkey NOUN a prison officer; jailer ❏ *As we came out of the prison through the lodge, I found that the great importance of my guardian was appreciated by the turnkeys, no less than by those whom they held in charge.* (*Great Expectations* by Charles Dickens)

turnpike NOUN the upkeep of many roads of the time was paid for by tolls (fees) collected at posts along the road. There was a gate to prevent people travelling further along the road until the toll had been paid. ❏ *Traddles, whom I have taken up by appointment at the turnpike, presents a dazzling combination of cream colour and light blue; and both he and Mr. Dick have a general effect about them of being all gloves.* (*David Copperfield* by Charles Dickens)

'twas PHRASE it was ❏ *'twas but a dream of thee* (*The Good-Morrow* by John Donne)

tyrannized VERB tyrannized means bullied or forced to do things against their will ❏ *for people would soon cease coming there to be tyrannized over and put down* (*Treasure Island* by Robert Louis Stevenson)

'un NOUN 'un is a slang term for one— usually used to refer to a person ❏ *She's been thinking the old 'un* (*David Copperfield* by Charles Dickens)

undistinguished ADJ undiscriminating or incapable of making a distinction between good and bad things ❑ *their undistinguished appetite to devour everything* (*Gulliver's Travels* by Jonathan Swift)

use NOUN habit ❑ *Though use make you apt to kill me* (*The Flea* by John Donne)

vacant ADJ vacant usually means empty, but here Wordsworth uses it to mean carefree ❑ *To vacant musing, unreproved neglect* (*The Prelude* by William Wordsworth)

valetudinarian NOUN one too concerned with his or her own health. ❑ *for having been a valetudinarian all his life* (*Emma* by Jane Austen)

vamp VERB vamp means to walk or tramp to somewhere ❑ *Well, vamp on to Marlott, will 'ee* (*Tess of the D'Urbervilles* by Thomas Hardy)

vapours NOUN the vapours is an old term which means unpleasant and strange thoughts, which make the person feel nervous and unhappy ❑ *and my head was full of vapours* (*Robinson Crusoe* by Daniel Defoe)

vegetables NOUN here vegetables means plants ❑ *the other vegetables are in the same proportion* (*Gulliver's Travels* by Jonathan Swift)

venturesome ADJ if you are venturesome you are willing to take risks ❑ *he must be either hopelessly stupid or a venturesome fool* (*Wuthering Heights* by Emily Brontë)

verily ADJ verily means really or truly ❑ *though I believe verily* (*Robinson Crusoe* by Daniel Defoe)

vicinage NOUN vicinage is an area or the residents of an area ❑ *and to his thought the whole vicinage was haunted by her.* (*Silas Marner* by George Eliot)

victuals NOUN victuals means food ❑ *grumble a little over the victuals* (*The Adventures of Huckleberry Finn* by Mark Twain)

vintage NOUN vintage in this context means wine ❑ *Oh, for a draught of*

vintage! (*Ode on a Nightingale* by John Keats)

virtual ADJ here virtual means powerful or strong ❑ *had virtual faith* (*The Prelude* by William Wordsworth)

vittles NOUN vittles is a slang word which means food ❑ *There never was such a woman for givin' away vittles and drink* (*Little Women* by Louisa May Alcott)

voided straight PHRASE voided straight is an old expression which means emptied immediately ❑ *see the rooms be voided straight* (*Doctor Faustus 4.1* by Christopher Marlowe)

wainscot NOUN wainscot is wood panel lining in a room so wainscoted means a room lined with wooden panels ❑ *in the dark wainscoted parlor* (*Silas Marner* by George Eliot)

walking the plank PHRASE walking the plank was a punishment in which a prisoner would be made to walk along a plank on the side of the ship and fall into the sea, where they would be abandoned ❑ *about hanging, and walking the plank* (*Treasure Island* by Robert Louis Stevenson)

want VERB want means to be lacking or short of ❑ *The next thing wanted was to get the picture framed* (*Emma* by Jane Austen)

wanting ADJ wanting means lacking or missing ❑ *wanting two fingers of the left hand* (*Treasure Island* by Robert Louis Stevenson)

wanting, I was not PHRASE I was not wanting means I did not fail ❑ *I was not wanting to lay a foundation of religious knowledge in his mind* (*Robinson Crusoe* by Daniel Defoe)

ward NOUN a ward is, usually, a child who has been put under the protection of the court or a guardian for his or her protection ❑ *I call the Wards in Jarndcye. The* are caged up with all the others. (*Bleak House* by Charles Dickens)

waylay VERB to waylay someone is to lie in wait for them or to intercept them ❑ *I must go up the road and waylay him* (*The Adventures of Huckleberry Finn* by Mark Twain)

weazen NOUN weazen is a slang word for throat. It actually means shrivelled ❑ *You with a uncle too! Why, I knowed you at Gargery's when you was so small a wolf that I could have took your weazen betwixt this finger and thumb and chucked you away dead* (*Great Expectations* by Charles Dickens)

wery ■ ADV very ❑ *Be wery careful o' vidders all your life* (*Pickwick Papers* by Charles Dickens) ■ *See* wibrated

wherry NOUN wherry is a small swift rowing boat for one person ❑ *It was flood tide when Daniel Quilp sat himself down in the wherry to cross to the opposite shore.* (*The Old Curiosity Shop* by Charles Dickens)

whether PREP whether means which of the two in this example ❑ *we came in full view of a great island and continent (for we knew not whether)* (*Gulliver's Travels* by Jonathan Swift)

whetstone NOUN a whetstone is a stone used to sharpen knives and other tools ❑ *I dropped pap's whetstone there too* (*The Adventures of Huckleberry Finn* by Mark Twain)

wibrated VERB in Dickens's use of the English language 'w' often replaces 'v' when he is reporting speech. So here 'wibrated' means 'vibrated'. In Pickwick Papers a judge asks Sam Weller (who constantly confuses the two letters) 'Do you spell it with a 'v' or a 'w'?' to which Weller replies 'That depends upon the taste and fancy of the speller, my Lord' ❑ *There are strings . . . in the human heart that had better not be wibrated*' (*Barnaby Rudge* by Charles Dickens)

wicket NOUN a wicket is a little door in a larger entrance ❑ *Having rested here, for a minute or so, to collect a*

good burst of sobs and an imposing show of tears and terror, he knocked loudly at the wicket; (*Oliver Twist* by Charles Dickens)

without CONJ without means unless ❑ *You don't know about me, without you have read a book by the name of The Adventures of Tom Sawyer* (*The Adventures of Huckleberry Finn* by Mark Twain)

wittles ■ NOUN vittles is a slang word which means food ❑ *I live on broken wittles–and I sleep on the coals* (*David Copperfield* by Charles Dickens) ■ *See* wibrated

woo VERB courts or forms a proper relationship with ❑ *before it woo* (*The Flea* by John Donne)

words, to have PHRASE if you have words with someone you have a disagreement or an argument ❑ *I do not want to have words with a young thing like you.* (*Black Beauty* by Anna Sewell)

workhouse NOUN workhouses were places where the homeless were given food and a place to live in return for doing very hard work ❑ *And the Union workhouses? demanded Scrooge. Are they still in operation?* (*A Christmas Carol* by Charles Dickens)

yawl NOUN a yawl is a small boat kept on a bigger boat for short trips. Yawl is also the name for a small fishing boat ❑ *She sent out her yawl, and we went aboard* (*The Adventures of Huckleberry Finn* by Mark Twain)

yeomanry NOUN the yeomanry was a collective term for the middle classes involved in agriculture ❑ *The yeomanry are precisely the order of people with whom I feel I can have nothing to do* (*Emma* by Jane Austen)

yonder ADV yonder means over there ❑ *all in the same second we seem to hear low voices in yonder!* (*The Adventures of Huckleberry Finn* by Mark Twain)